LEAP OF FAITH

Chest burning, Joe tore across the wide expanse of concrete in the unfinished building, Frank right at his side. Behind them, they could hear George mounting the stairs. They'd never reach the far side of the building.

Then Frank was grabbing Joe's arm, pulling him off course. He led him to a set of large square holes in the floor, set in the middle of the building. Without letting go of Joe, Frank threw himself over the edge.

As they dropped, a gunshot rang out over their heads.

Joe closed his eyes. . . .

Books in THE HARDY BOYS CASEFILES® Series

Case #1 DEAD ON TARGET
Case #2 EVIL, INC.
Case #3 CULT OF CRIME
Case #4 THE LAZARUS PLOT
Case #5 EDGE OF DESTRUCTION
Case #6 THE CROWNING TERROR
Case #7 DEATHGAME
Case #8 SEE NO EVIL
Case #9 THE GENIUS THIEVES
Case #10 HOSTAGES OF HATE
Case #11 BROTHER AGAINST BROTHER
Case #12 PERFECT GETAWAY
Case #13 THE BORGIA DAGGER
Case #14 TOO MANY TRAITORS
Case #15 BLOOD RELATIONS
Case #16 LINE OF FIRE

Available from ARCHWAY Paperbacks

THE HARDY BOYS CASEFILES NO. 16

LINE OF FIRE

FRANKLIN W. DIXON

AN ARCHWAY PAPERBACK
Published by POCKET BOOKS
New York   London   Toronto   Sydney   Tokyo

AN ARCHWAY PAPERBACK *Original*

An Archway Paperback published by
POCKET BOOKS, a divison of Simon & Schuster Inc.
1230 Avenue of the Americas, New York, N.Y. 10020

ISBN: 0-671-64462-9

First Archway Paperback printing June 1988

10 9 8 7 6 5 4 3 2 1

LINE OF FIRE

Chapter

1

"YOU'VE GOT THE wrong guy!" Joe Hardy raised his hands. More than two dozen expectant faces had turned to watch him as he walked in the door. "Save all the shouting until Denny, the real birthday boy, comes in."

Joe brushed back his unruly blond hair with one hand and grinned when he finally spotted his older brother. Naturally, Frank had chosen a quiet corner with a good view of the whole living room. He was talking with his girlfriend, Callie Shaw, their heads close together.

They both looked up as Joe worked his way toward them through the crowd. "This is going to be some bash," Joe said. "Denny Payson's a lucky guy. I hope you guys are taking notes. It would be nice to have a surprise party when *I* turn eighteen.''

Callie laughed. ''It won't be much of a surprise if you're all ready for it.''

''Besides,'' Frank added, ''I thought you didn't like surprises anymore—not after last time.'' Their last case, *Blood Relations,* had taken some nasty twists that had almost killed the Hardys.

''Well, I wouldn't mind a *nice* surprise, like Bonnie dancing only with me tonight.'' Joe nodded toward the middle of the room, where a gorgeous girl with long red hair sat. Four guys were falling all over themselves to get her sodas and snacks.

Frank's grin got bigger. ''That wouldn't be a surprise. It would be a miracle.''

The two brothers looked very different from each other. Joe, with his blond good looks and sparkling blue eyes, was a little shorter than Frank. He was the stockier of the two, with muscles stretching the chest of his sport shirt. Frank was leaner, with dark hair and eyes, and a deep tan from the summer sun.

Yet, as they both turned simultaneously and their eyes narrowed to watch someone approach, they seemed almost identical.

''Hi, Mrs. Payson,'' Joe said, recognizing the hostess of the party.

''Hello, boys.'' Elizabeth Payson put a hand

on each of their shoulders. "I'm so glad you could make it."

Frank gave her a smile. "This party is the hot event of the summer. Every kid in town is buzzing about it."

"And trying to keep the secret from getting out to Denny," Joe added. "Where is our guest of honor?"

"Barbara was taking him out so we could get things ready," Mrs. Payson explained, smiling at a photo on the mantel.

It was a picture from the junior prom. Denny had his arm around his girlfriend, Barbara Lynch. Her petite frame and dark hair contrasted with the tall, redheaded Denny. He was grinning in the picture, and Frank, Joe, and Callie unconsciously smiled back.

"It's so good to see Denny smiling again," Mrs. Payson said. "And I wanted this to be a special birthday, to wipe out some of the other memories."

Five years before, just as Denny was turning thirteen, his father and three other men had died in the big fire at the Crowell Chemical plant. It had been the most tragic fire in Bayport history.

For the Paysons, it had been a complete disaster. Without Mr. Payson, they had no income, and stood to lose their house, their furniture, everything.

But the people of Bayport, led by Lucius

3

Crowell, had rallied round. Crowell, the owner of the plant, had been the hero of the fire, risking his life to rescue the trapped men. Frank and Joe both remembered Crowell's picture in the newspaper, his face and clothes smudged with smoke as he led a worker out of the inferno.

Lucius Crowell had organized a drive to raise money for the widows and children. He set up a fund to save their homes and take care of the kids' educations. He'd been like an uncle to Denny ever since.

Mrs. Payson glanced at her watch. "I wonder what's keeping them? Barbara should have had him back by now."

"Um," said Joe, "I'm sure they'll be here soon. Oh, by the way, I've got a present for Denny. Are you putting them anyplace special?"

The kids followed Mrs. Payson to a table piled high with packages.

"It's a new book about target pistols," Joe went on. "I saw it the last time I was in the city and picked it up then." He smoothed one of the edges on the thick, sloppily wrapped package. "Hope he hasn't got it already."

Smiling, Mrs. Payson took the package. "I'm sure he'll love it."

"Well, I thought it would be right for Dead-Eye Denny." Joe used the nickname the Bayport *Times* had given Denny after he won his

4

last pistol competition. Denny's superior abilities as a marksman were responsible for his getting his picture on sports pages all over the state.

Joe leaned forward as Mrs. Payson put his package on top of the pile. He'd just noticed that one of the presents was unwrapped. At the front of the table, propped up in a special presentation case, was a customized target pistol.

"Hey, that's some gun." Joe whistled as he took in the clean lines of the automatic pistol. It was an old-fashioned Army Colt, but it had been reworked for competition. Most of the exposed metal was chrome plated. A specially weighted and vented muzzle shroud had been added for extra accuracy. There was even a special trigger.

And clamped to the top of the Colt was a high-tech gunsight that made Frank take a second look. "Is that—" he began.

"A laser sight," a voice boomed behind him. "My present for Denny."

They all turned to see Lucius Crowell standing behind them, a big smile on his face. He was a little heavier than the hero in the newspaper photos, and a lot slicker-looking now.

His hair rose in carefully rumpled curls that tried to hide his receding hairline. The trademark bushy mustache he had always worn was now carefully trimmed. But the slightly oversize features of his face were still handsome, and his suit fit his stocky form perfectly. Now that Joe thought about it, the only time he'd seen Crowell out of a suit and tie was on the night of the big fire.

Crowell carried one reminder of the fire: the sturdy cane he was leaning on. He'd gone back into the blaze once too often, trying to save Denny's father, and was injured when the roof collapsed.

But that memory was long behind him as Crowell told Frank about the gunsight. "Since I knew Elizabeth was getting the custom gun for Denny, I had them add this little piece of hardware. It's one of the new generation of microlaser sights," he said. "It weighs only half a pound, and it's good for almost a hundred yards. The laser plants a little red dot that shows where the bullet will go."

"Amazing," Frank said.

"I can hardly wait to see the results," Crowell went on. "The sight is excellent for quick targeting, and I'm sure it'll help Denny a lot. We may yet be seeing him on an Olympic team. And think what that would mean to Bayport."

Joe whispered to Frank, "The way he says 'Bayport,' you'd think he'd invented the town."

"It's the election," Frank whispered back. "That's the way all the politicians talk just before an election."

The special election for town supervisor was coming close, and the campaign had heated up. Lucius Crowell was the front-runner.

"He's about the only public figure in town with clean hands," Frank went on. Corruption and scandal had rocked the local government after the Hardys proved that Jack Morrison, the former supervisor, had been murdered by some of his crooked associates in their *See No Evil* case.

Joe grinned. "Well, I know one person who's sure to vote for him—Denny turned eighteen at just the right time."

"Speaking of Denny," Lucius Crowell was saying to Mrs. Payson, "are you sure you told Barbara the right time?"

She gave another worried look at her watch. "I told her to bring him back by seven-thirty. It's way after that now. . . ."

At that moment, the front door opened. Barbara Lynch walked in. She turned and looked nervously at the lanky boy who was now standing framed in the doorway.

Denny Payson had been frowning as he stepped in. He stopped, blinking in astonishment as everyone yelled, "Surprise!"

The frown quickly returned to his face after he scanned the crowd and his gaze stopped beside Frank, Joe, and Callie.

He roughly pushed his way through the

crowd, ignoring all the kids who were trying to congratulate him and shake his hand.

Then he halted just past Frank to confront Lucius Crowell.

"I've just learned the truth about you, you hypocrite!" Denny shouted. "You killed my father!"

Chapter

2

JOE HARDY STARED out the side window of the van as the Payson house disappeared from sight. "That was about the shortest party I've ever been to," he said to Frank and Callie.

Frank glanced over at him as he turned onto the highway. "There wasn't anything to celebrate after Denny and Lucius Crowell got finished yelling at each other."

"The person I felt sorriest for was Mrs. Payson," Callie said, shifting in her seat. "She had to listen to her son scream at the man who did so much to help them. And then watch Mr. Crowell storm out and everybody else slink off. Poor Mrs. Payson. I bet she's stuck with enough food to feed an army."

"And cake," Joe added mournfully. "I won-

9

der if they were going to have chocolate birthday cake."

"You're beginning to sound like Chet Morton," Frank said, kidding him. "What I wonder is how this will affect the election."

Callie looked at him. "You think it will?"

Joe began to look interested. "Denny accused Crowell of murder, in front of a whole roomful of people. They're sure to talk. It'll be all over town soon."

"But it doesn't make sense!" Callie protested. "Crowell didn't murder Mr. Payson. He tried to save him."

"Denny didn't say anything about murder," Frank cut in. " 'I've just learned the truth about you. . . .' " he murmured, repeating Denny's words. " 'You killed my father.' "

Joe shrugged. "Killed, murdered. What's the difference?"

"Denny wasn't accusing Crowell of shooting his father, or anything as direct as that," Frank said. "He's got to be talking about the fire where his father died."

Callie looked disbelieving. "So? Did Crowell set the fire?"

"I can't see it happening like that." Frank frowned. "But what if the disaster turned out not to be an accident? What if it could've been prevented? That fire is what made Lucius Crowell a hero and big man in this town. Suppose it turned out to be his fault, though . . .''

"That would be hot news—*especially* if he's running for town supervisor." For a second, Joe looked excited, then his eyes narrowed. "Wait a minute, if he'd done something to cause the fire, why hasn't it ever come out? It would have been hot news five years ago."

"Maybe he covered it up," Callie said. "He sure looked furious when Denny started in on him at the party. I thought he was going to pick up that gun on the table."

"It was close," Frank agreed. "Except my money would have been on Denny. He actually looked over at the gun for a second."

"I just hope it all turns out okay." Callie sounded worried. "Crowell is rich and powerful. And Denny is standing up to him all alone."

"If he needs help—" Frank and Joe both began to speak, stopped, looked at each other, and laughed.

Callie started laughing too. "What's the matter, guys? No cases lately?"

At that moment they had reached Callie's block. Frank brought the van to a stop in front of her house.

Callie leaned over and kissed Frank goodbye. "Night, guys." She popped out the door and headed up the walk.

Frank pulled away. "Where to?"

Joe shrugged. "Home, I guess."

They had just come through the door when the telephone began ringing. Joe grabbed the phone and grinned as soon as he said hello.

"Hey, Callie, couldn't get enough of us, huh?" But his eyebrows went up as he listened. Then he handed the phone to Frank.

"Were you guys serious when you said you'd help Denny?" Callie asked.

"Well, *I* was serious about helping him," Frank said. He repeated her question to Joe, who nodded. "Why?"

"I just got a call from Barbara Lynch," Callie said. "She thinks Denny has bitten off more than he can chew."

"Maybe Barbara thinks so. But does Denny think so? Last time we saw him, he didn't look in a mood to take anyone's advice," Frank said.

"She wants us to stop by the Payson place tomorrow," Callie said. "What do you say?"

Frank shrugged. "We've got nothing planned," he said. "I don't mind going over to the Payson place—as long as Denny doesn't come out armed."

But as they stepped out of the van the next morning, the first thing they heard was a gunshot.

Barbara appeared from around the side of the house. "Denny is out back, test-firing that new pistol," she explained.

They followed her to the backyard. The Payson house was on the outskirts of Bayport, without any houses close. And the yard continued back for at least a hundred yards. It was bounded by woods on three sides.

With all this space, Denny had no problem setting up his own shooting range. A rough dirt wall acted as his backstop, ready to catch any stray bullets.

In front of the wall stretched two lines of targets—eight-inch metal plates spaced a foot apart. White paint glistened even though the day was overcast.

Denny stood about ten yards from the targets. The pistol they'd seen the night before was in his right hand, its muzzle pointed straight up. He brought it down to eye level, his left hand cupped around his right to brace it.

A beam of brilliant red light shot from the futuristic sight mounted on top of the gun. Pencil thin, it pinpointed the exact center of the first white plate. Denny fired, and the plate flopped back.

His hands moved, the beam flicked to the next plate, and Denny fired again. The beam flicked to the next target and the next. With six quick shots, Denny had nailed all the targets.

13

The gun pointed skyward again, Denny whirled around, grinning. Then he faltered when he saw he had company.

"That was some shooting," Joe said enthusiastically. "No wonder you're a champ."

Denny looked a little embarrassed. "I suppose I shouldn't be using this to practice—at least with the sight. It makes it too easy, and then I get lazy." Then he grinned like a little boy with a new toy. "But I couldn't help trying it out."

"You were very impressive," Frank said, stepping up to inspect the gun more closely. "Six for six—and pretty quick."

"That was standing on top of them," Denny said. "In real competition, you just *start* shooting at ten yards."

He pointed over to a table. "I set that up at twenty-five yards for a real practice shoot. Want to help?"

"Sure." Joe stood beside the rough wooden table. It held a two-liter bottle of soda, some glasses, a few loose bullets, and two loaded clips for the pistol.

Denny dropped the clip out of his gun and worked the action. "Empty," he said. Putting the gun on the table, he trotted over to the metal plates, setting them up again.

He smiled as he returned to find Frank gazing intently at the gun sight. "I forgot how interested you are in high-tech stuff," Denny said. Picking the pistol up by the barrel, he handed it to Frank. "Go ahead, check it out. The gun's empty."

Even so, Frank checked the action again. Denny nodded approvingly. "I heard that you guys knew something about guns. What do you think of this baby?"

"A little heavy," Frank said, hefting the gun. "But not as heavy as I expected."

"Just try holding it with your arms out for a little while," Denny said. "After only a minute it feels like it weighs a ton."

Frank looked at a small pressure switch at the back of the handgrip. "Is that the control for the laser?"

"You got it," Denny said. "Why not give it a try?"

Frank sighted down the range and squeezed the little control. The red beam stabbed out of the gun sight, painting an inch-wide red dot on the edge of one of the plates.

"Not bad," said Denny.

"Well, at least I hit the one I was aiming at—barely." Frank released the control, and the red light winked out. "And that's exactly where my bullet would have gone?"

"Not exactly. The farther back you go, the more things you have to take into consideration.

The light beam goes straight ahead, but the bullet's trajectory is curved."

Frank nodded. "I think it might have gone under the plate."

Denny shrugged. "You'd need just a little practice."

"I also saw that the dot on the plate was bigger. How much does the beam diffuse?"

"It's only good for about a hundred yards and you can't use it in bright daylight," Denny said. "But other than that, it can be a big help."

He took the gun from Frank's hand, picked up a clip, and slapped it into the butt of the gun. "Want to time me? I get nine seconds to get all twelve plates."

Frank nodded and held up his wristwatch. "Okay. I'll tell you when to start."

Joe picked up the bottle of soda and a glass from the table. "Well, if I'm going to be a spectator, I'm going to get myself some refreshments."

Denny hardly seemed to listen as he put the gun back on the table. He stood with his hands at shoulder height.

Frank watched the second hand creep up to the twelve. "Now!" he called.

Moving smoothly, Denny's right hand swept the gun up, his left working the action. He took the brace position, and the laser winked into existence. One shot, and the left-most plate fell down.

Two more shots, and two more plates fell down. Denny jerked toward the next, and his shot missed. Shaking his head, he bore down harder, spacing his shots more carefully.

The fourth, fifth, sixth, and seventh plates fell, one shot to each. But Denny had used up all the bullets in his clip. He ejected the empty clip and started to reach for the full one on the table.

As he did that, another circle of red winked onto the next plate. It was much larger—four inches wide—and it didn't come from Denny's sight.

Joe whirled around, to see another laser beam shining from the woods to the side of them—a good hundred yards away. Even as he was turning, he heard a gun firing.

Five shots cracked in quick succession, knocking down the remaining plates. Then came a sixth, and that one knocked Joe down!

Chapter

3

FRANK THREW HIMSELF down, then began wriggling across to Joe. Callie, Denny, and Barbara had all dropped flat, trying to stay below the hidden gunman's line of fire.

Frank stayed low as he continued to snake his way to Joe's side. "Joe," he whispered, reaching out and fingering the large wet stain on his brother's shirt.

"Don't sweat it." Joe grinned up at his brother. "That's root beer. Nothing wrong with me except maybe a bruise or two. *This* is what got hit."

He held up the two-liter-size plastic soda bottle. Two holes showed where the bullet had passed through. Soda was still leaking out.

"That shot packed quite a wallop," Joe said. "Nearly tore the bottle right out of my hand."

"So instead you held on and let it knock you flat on your back." Frank shook his head in exasperation.

Both Hardys turned as Denny Payson snatched a clip of bullets from the table. No more shots came from the woods as he slapped the magazine into the gun still gripped in his hand. He jumped to his feet, aiming the pistol at the woods.

"Hold it a second," said Joe. "We all saw how well that guy shoots. And you want to go charging across this open yard into the woods where he's hiding?"

"You're going to let him get away, after he shot at us?" Denny stared at the Hardys in disbelief.

"There was no shot when you grabbed that clip. He's probably gone already." Frank frowned thoughtfully as he stared at the woods in the distance. "And he wasn't shooting at us."

"You could have fooled me," said Callie. "Were those spitballs flying past us?"

"No, they were bullets," Frank said. "But as you just said, they flew past. That guy was shooting *around* us." He pointed at the downed plates and the wounded soda bottle. "With that sight, he was able to put a bullet into each of these targets, which are a lot smaller than we are. If he'd wanted to, he could have nailed all of us."

"So why didn't he?" Denny challenged.

"Because he didn't want to," Frank answered coolly. "Or, more likely, he'd been *told* not to." He stared at Denny's pale face. "This was a warning, something to let you know the kind of trouble you've let yourself in for."

"I can handle it." Denny's jaw stuck out, and he gripped his gun tighter.

"Looks like you could use some help," Joe put in.

Barbara Lynch looked nervously at her boyfriend. "Denny—" she began.

"Don't *you* start too, Barb," Denny burst out. He glared at the Hardys. "I don't need any help, in spite of what you all think." Turning his back on them, he stared off at the woods. "And I really don't need help that tells me to wimp out when some guy shoots at me. I thought the Hardy brothers had a better rep than that."

Joe opened his mouth to answer, but Frank shut him up with a look.

"Now, thanks to your so-called advice, you've kept me here while that guy got away." Denny rose to his feet, his gun ready. He started stalking toward the woods in a combat crouch. "If you want to help so much, why don't you do something useful, like call the cops?" he threw over his shoulder.

Frank got up and took a step after him. "We shouldn't let him go alone."

Barbara Lynch took his arm. *"One* of you can go with him. There's something upstairs I want you to see."

Joe shrugged. "You go take a look. I'll baby-sit Captain Commando." He took off across the yard as Barbara led Frank and Callie into the house.

"Mrs. Payson is out at the mall, shopping," Barbara explained as they entered the house through a basement door.

"Probably just as well," Frank said, glancing around a neat, carefully tended workshop. He gazed at a vaguely familiar piece of equipment clamped to a workbench.

"A reloading machine!" he said with interest. "So, Denny doesn't just shoot, he makes his own bullets. He must be a fanatic."

"Fanatic," Barbara echoed. She started up the stairs. "A good way to describe Denny. I never really thought about that, until—well, I'll let you see."

They followed her to the first floor, where Callie went to the phone to call the police. But Barbara beckoned to Frank, continuing on to the second floor, and one of the bedrooms—Denny's, from the look of it.

"I think you should have a look at this. Since Denny's out beating the bushes, this is a good chance.'' She pointed at the desk facing the bedroom window—and the thick scrapbook sitting on it.

Frank sat at the desk and began turning pages. They were covered with newspaper clippings, all about the Crowell Chemical disaster. He saw pictures of the firemen fighting the flames, the shot of the smoky Lucius Crowell leading a worker to safety, and portraits of the men who had lost their lives, including Mr. Payson.

He went on through the pages, finding maps and diagrams, then stories about the building of a new, modern Crowell plant. "He must have everything that was ever printed about the fire and Crowell Chemical. There are even stories about Lucius Crowell's campaign for supervisor." He flipped through the book again. "And the pages are pretty worn. He must go over them a lot."

"All the time," Barbara said. "He keeps reading and rereading those stories, still trying to make sense of it all."

The scrapbook fell open to one page. It was a story about the lost workers. Lined up at the top were five photos, evidently collected from their families. Frank looked from the picture of Mr. Payson smiling up at him to the wall, where the same picture was framed.

Over it hung a long-barreled pistol. "A plinking gun," Barbara said, following Frank's eyes.

"Denny's last present from his dad. They used to go out in the forest and knock over tin cans."

She took a deep breath. "The two biggest things in Denny's life are his shooting and what he calls the mystery of the fire. Everything else takes second place, even me. I mean, I love him, and he loves me. But—well, yesterday proved it."

Frank shut the book. "What got him started on Mr. Crowell?"

Barbara shook her head. "I don't know. I was supposed to take him out, so Mrs. Payson could get ready for the party. We went downtown first, to the town hall to look at some records—"

"Then to the county and state offices, and then over to the federal center?" Frank asked.

Barbara stared. "How did you—?"

"I should have guessed. It makes sense, now that I've seen this," Frank tapped the scrapbook. "Denny's been collecting everything he can get his hands on about the Crowell fire. He just turned eighteen. That means he can finally get access to government files. I'll bet he wrote letters months in advance, setting up those visits. And whatever he saw—"

Frank abruptly cut himself off and got up from the desk. "I can see Denny coming back. Don't tell him you told us, okay?"

"Are you kidding?" Barbara said. "If he found out, he'd kill me."

"I'd hate to put it that way," Frank said, heading downstairs.

As they reached the first floor, the phone began to ring. Callie picked it up. "Just wait a second," she said as Denny came in the front door.

Callie held out the phone. "For you."

Denny took it, listened for a moment, then began to shout. "You're not going to scare me off, and you can tell that to your boss. People besides me are starting to ask for a grand jury investigation. And I can prove—"

He stared at the phone for a second, listening, then yelled, "You'll do *what?* You slimy—"

White-faced, he smashed the handset down on its cradle.

"That was the guy who shot at me. He described it all. Told me I should forget about making stupid accusations."

Joe nodded. "That's when you began shouting, I guess."

"I'm more interested in what he said to make you shut up," Frank said.

"He told me I might not be the only one to get hurt if I keep on going," Denny said. "Asked if I wasn't alone enough in the world as it was."

Callie sucked in her breath.

"Sounds like a really nice guy," Joe said quietly.

"I don't care—" Denny began.

"Well, you'd better *start* caring," Frank cut him off. "You're in a game where the other side plays dirty, and you can't win all by yourself."

"So I should put myself in your hands, the way my mom let Crowell take over our lives?" Denny was about to go on when a loud creaking sounded outside.

"Old board on the porch," Denny whispered as he homed in on the sound. He moved the target pistol up easily, like a natural extension of his body.

Joe slipped silently to the side of the door and reached out to grasp the doorknob. Frank herded the girls to the other side, out of the line of fire.

Then Joe threw the door open, revealing a tall figure in a police uniform, about to knock on the door.

The man caught sight of Denny, yelled, "What the—?" and went into a crouch.

With one hand he grabbed the door and pulled it closed again.

While his other hand streaked for the gun in his holster.

Chapter

4

"HOLD IT!" FRANK Hardy yelled at the top of his lungs. He leapt on Denny, wrestling his gun upward. "Joe, open the door slowly. Con Riley's out there!"

The door swung open again, this time revealing Patrolman Con Riley and his partner, both in firing positions.

"Get away from him, Frank," Con called out. Con Riley was the Hardys' closest friend on the force. And there he was, aiming a gun at Frank.

"Take it easy," Frank said. "It's not what it looks like."

Denny let go of his gun, and Frank stepped back, holding it out butt-first.

Con Riley came through the door. He hadn't put his gun away. "I get a report of somebody engaged in some illegal shooting at this address. With a ray gun, no less. Why am I not surprised to find the Hardys involved in this? Someone want to tell me what's going on around here?" he asked.

"Somebody tried to kill us!" Denny exclaimed. "And he just called, making more threats."

Slowly Riley looked around the room, and finally holstered his pistol. "Okay, Frank, how about *you* filling me in—without getting excited about it?"

Frank reported what had happened out in the backyard, with Joe filling him in on the search through the woods.

Riley's eyes narrowed. "You found nothing, you say? No spent shells?"

Joe shurgged. "Nothing there. Either he was using a revolver, or he cleaned up after himself."

"And this threatening phone call?"

"I answered the phone," Callie said.

"And did you hear any threats?"

Callie shook her head. "Um—no. Denny heard them."

Riley looked at Denny. "Very convenient. Threats that only you can hear."

Denny's face tightened. "And I suppose *I* fired those shots at us too?"

"It wouldn't be too hard for you to arrange,"

27

Riley suggested. "A guy like you would have lots of friends who could shoot like that. And a little stunt like this"—he looked over at the Hardys and smiled—"with the right kind of witnesses, would really help any stories you might want to tell."

"Stories?" Denny repeated.

"Let's just say that a lot of people have heard about your, uh, conversation with Mr. Crowell."

"Oh, I get it," Denny said. "And Crowell's been at work trying to make me look bad so I won't harm his precious reputation. Is that it?"

"Make you look bad?" said Riley. "I don't know how he could do that. I mean, lots of people answer their doors with guns in their hands. Right?"

"Well, you've got one way to clear out a lot of suspects," Frank put in. "This guy's gun was equipped with a laser sight. He used it when aiming his shots."

Riley nodded. "A laser sight. That's the kind competition marksmen use."

"It might be interesting to see if anyone else in town has one," Frank suggested.

"It might be," Riley admitted. "Now, about this firearm . . ." He reached out his hand for the Colt that Frank was now holding.

"Hey, you can't take my gun!" Denny burst out.

"Sure I can. Don't you remember? You were about to use it to plug a police officer."

"Hey, Con, lighten up a little, will you?" Joe said, earning himself a dirty look from the policeman.

Frank spoke up. "You're perfectly right, Con. Of course, you'll be putting this house under police protection."

Riley stared at Frank. "Why?"

"Well, you've heard about the attack here. So I hope you won't leave this isolated house defenseless, just in case someone comes out and uses it for target practice."

Riley stopped reaching for the pistol. "Okay, keep the gun," he said to Denny. "But use your head before you draw it again!" He pulled out a notebook. "Now, I'll need to get a full statement from you . . ."

"Do you think that maybe Con didn't exactly believe Denny's story?" Joe said as he, Frank, and Callie finally drove off. The police had left only moments before.

"What gave you that idea?" Callie asked. "The way Con Riley cross-examined him whenever he opened his mouth?"

"Well, it did make me a little suspicious," Joe admitted, poker-faced. "That, and the way Con tried so hard to get something out of us to contradict him."

They laughed, but Frank didn't join in. "It's not so funny," he said. "Denny's made himself a powerful enemy. Lucius Crowell is a real pillar of the community. The cops aren't ready to take Denny's word against his, and Denny isn't helping any. Every time he opens his mouth, his accusations get a little wilder."

"You don't think Con could be right, do you?" Joe asked. "That Denny got a friend to help set us up to go after Crowell? Maybe I'm getting suspicious in my old age. But it reminds me of Mike and Greg in our last case."

Frank shook his head. "I believe Denny is dead serious about getting to the bottom of whatever caused the Crowell Chemical disaster." He explained about the detailed scrapbook Barbara had shown him, and Denny's visits to uncover the old government records.

"Whatever Denny found in there has set him against Lucius Crowell," Frank went on. "And as far as tricking us to help him—well, before we left, he took me off to the side. In no uncertain terms, he told me that he doesn't want us sticking our noses in."

"Funny," Callie said. "Barbara pulled me aside and begged for any help we could give Denny."

"Well, before we make up our minds, we'll have to do some digging." Frank turned to Callie. "Do you think Liz Webling will be at the offices of the Bayport *Times?*"

Liz was a friend of Callie's, and her father was editor of the newspaper. "I want to see what they've got on Lucius Crowell—and Denny. Denny said he had proof that Crowell was behind the disaster at the factory. Maybe he passed it along to the *Times.*"

Callie nodded. "They'll be putting the paper to bed soon. Liz is probably there," she said. "Drop me off at the office."

Frank nodded and drove the van downtown. As soon as Callie hopped out, Joe turned to his brother. "While Callie's digging, what are we going to do?"

"Why don't we check out Lucius Crowell?"

As they headed out toward the mansion district, Joe kept noticing the campaign posters in store windows. Lots of people were running for supervisor. But more posters had Lucius Crowell's face on them. Each one carried the message: "Luke Crowell—Clean Leadership for Bayport."

"Luke?" Joe said, staring out of the window.

"That's to show he's a man of the people. *Lucius* sounds too upper class."

Joe shook his head. "I think he's trying a little too hard."

"Maybe you'll have a chance to tell him

that," Frank said as he turned into the driveway of one of the bigger mansions.

Two tall wrought-iron gates blocked their way. They could hear video cameras whirring, focusing on Frank as he leaned out the window. He pressed a button on a box at the side of the gate.

A tinny voice came out. "Deliveries come in the service entrance."

"This isn't a delivery," Frank interrupted, his lips tightening. "We're here to see Mr. Crowell."

"Do you have an appointment?"

"No, but I think he'll see us. We've come to tell him that somebody has been taking shots at Denny Payson—if he doesn't know about it already."

There was no answer. The box simply went dead. Joe looked over at Frank. "You think he's gone?"

Frank's only answer was to put a finger to his lips.

They sat for a moment, listening to the breeze sighing through the tree branches. Then the tinny voice came through the box again. "Drive up to the front door. Mr. Crowell will see you."

Frank waited for the gates to swing open, and then he drove the van up the drive. He and Joe walked up to the dark green door, which was promptly opened.

"This way." The owner of the tinny voice was much more impressive in person. His voice was deep and a little hoarse, coming from a bull-like throat. He dwarfed Frank's six feet one inch, and his shoulders brushed either side of the doorway.

All the Hardys saw was muscle—swelling in his arms, straining the chest of his sport jacket. One of his cheeks had a scar—more like a dent, as if a chunk of muscle had been removed.

The man's hairline had receded halfway up his head, and he looked mean. "Follow me," he said.

As he led the way into the house, Joe noticed something else about their guide. Under the ill-fitting jacket was a distinctly unmuscular lump, certainly a pistol in a shoulder rig. And judging by the size of the lump, it had to be a pretty big pistol. Joe silently nudged Frank's elbow and pointed.

They arrived at what was either Crowell's den or library. Lucius Crowell rose from a heavy leather chair, and for once, he wasn't in a suit and tie. Frank blinked in disbelief. They'd never seen him in anything other than a suit, except the night of the fire. But right then Lucius Crowell wore a red silk dressing gown and print ascot.

"You came to tell me something about Denny?" he asked, looking at them. "Why do you think I should be interested?"

"You were interested enough to ask us in," Frank answered. "After we mentioned that someone shot at him."

Crowell's eyes flickered to the hulking character still standing in the doorway. "That'll be all, George. You may return to your duties."

Poker-faced, George disappeared.

"Not exactly your typical butler," Joe commented, looking after him.

"George does a lot of work for me," Crowell said, sitting down again. "Now, tell me about this so-called shooting."

"Oh, I expect you've already heard about it," Frank said, watching as Crowell's face froze. "I mean, after all, you've got friends on the police force. Somebody was sure to call you."

Crowell relaxed again. "But I'd like to hear your story."

"Oh, it's pretty simple." Frank told about the shots and the search. He didn't mention Denny's scrapbook. "Denny is convinced that someone is trying to scare him into silence," Frank concluded. "And I guess I don't need to tell you who he's blaming."

He stared at Lucius Crowell. "All of a sudden he's accusing you, who's always *helped* his family, of terrible things. Maybe he has found something, maybe he hasn't. We can't be sure of anything, except the shots and the phone call.

34

Maybe you know something we don't, and if you two talked it out . . ."

Lucius Crowell sat very quietly, his eyes closed. When he opened them, Frank saw that he had failed to convince him.

"Dennis and I have nothing to talk about. If you're a friend of his, you might tell him to watch out where he does his talking."

"Is that a threat?" Joe demanded.

Crowell turned to him. With his clenched jaw and glaring eyes, he resembled a frog.

"I thought Denny might have been scamming us—until now," Joe said. "We'll be watching out for him. Who knows—there may be a case here."

He looked Crowell straight in the eye. "And if there is a case, we'll get to the bottom of it. Remember the Morrison case. Of course, if there isn't one, then you have nothing to worry about." He grinned.

Crowell struggled to stay in control. "Is *that* a threat?" he asked.

Joe stared at him. "No, just a friendly warning," he said, heading for the door. "Come on, Frank." He stopped at the doorway and looked back at Crowell. "No need to call your 'butler.' We know our way out."

They walked out of the house, climbed into the van, and started off. The gates swung open automatically as they reached the end of the drive.

"Well, what did you think?" Joe asked.

"I'd hate to play poker with him," Frank said, turning the van onto the road. "He doesn't rattle easily, even when we put the pressure on."

"Yeah, but he is hiding something. Denny is right."

"That's what I think too, brother." Frank didn't sound excited, but Joe could see the gleam in his eyes. They had a case!

Almost unconsciously, Frank accelerated the van along a straightaway. The engine hummed as they took off.

Ahead of them, the road curved to the right.

Frank's foot was just reaching for the brake when a brilliant flash of red caught his eye in the rearview mirror. It was there for just an instant, then it was gone.

Frank had just turned his attention away from the mirror when he heard a muffled *crack*. He glanced up again but didn't see anything in the mirror.

He had other things to think about, anyway.

His left rear tire had blown, and the van was now careening wildly across the road!

Chapter

5

FRANK GRIPPED THE wheel harder, trying to steer with the skid and not against it. But now they were spinning wildly, totally out of control. It seemed there was no way they could stay on the road.

But if they didn't make the curve, they'd crash head-on into a brick wall. One of the mansion owners had apparently decided he didn't want passersby gawking at his grounds and had built a ten-foot-high brick wall around his place. Frank didn't know if it had discouraged gawking, but he knew what would happen if the van hit it. He and Joe would be pancakes.

Desperately, Frank tried to bring the van under control. The wall came closer as he forced the van to continue its skid. The wall blurred before their eyes. The van's bodywork groaned from the stress. If Frank miscalculated, they'd topple over. . . .

But riding the edges of the tires, Frank managed to keep them upright. With a thud the van fell back solidly on its wheels and tore across the gravel drive leading to a massive steel gate. Finally it plowed through some holly bushes and came to a stop, nosed up against the wall.

Joe let out a soft, shuddering breath. "That was a very bad time to get a flat," he finally said.

"It wasn't an accident." Frank pushed his door open and got out to look at the tire.

"What do you mean?" Joe jumped out and ran around the back to join him.

"It had help." Frank pointed at the wreckage of the tire. "This is where it tore apart—see this hole here."

Joe leaned forward. "Looks like a bullet hole."

"Exactly." Frank's face was grim. "I *thought* I saw a flash of red in the mirror."

"A laser sight? You mean Denny?"

"He's not the only one in town with that kind of sight," Frank said. "There's the guy who played target practice all around our heads."

"Denny is the only one *we* know," Joe pointed out. Then he shook his head. "But

Denny didn't know where we were going. Anyway, he'd never do something like that."

"And all the way into town, I had one eye on the rearview mirror. I'd have noticed if anyone was following us."

"So we're dealing with a deadly marksman who reads minds—or—"

"Or?" Frank said.

"Crowell's butler, George. He left after we came into the room, and we didn't see him on the way out. And he was toting a gun as big as a cannon under his jacket."

Frank nodded. "He'd know which way we'd be heading. And that curve in the road is just a short walk from Crowell's mansion." He sighed. "But even if he did shoot at us, he's probably back home by now—with a perfect alibi."

"You're right." Joe kicked the dead tire. "So how can we prove it, one way or the other?"

"We might put a word in Con Riley's ear. So he can check him out."

"Good idea." Joe grinned. Then his grin slipped. "But I bet that George's actions aren't going to be easy to trace."

Frank shrugged. "We can hope." Then he kicked the dead tire too. "We'd better change this and see about fixing the damage we did. After that, I want to give Callie a call at the *Times*."

Callie didn't have good news. "Liz is giving

me her investigative reporter act. She doesn't want to reveal her information or her source.''

Frank sighed. "We know her source, and the information will probably be in tomorrow's paper.''

"Maybe not. The reporters aren't having an easy time checking out all of the things Denny's saying. And since he's saying things about Lucius Crowell, they've got to be careful. It might not be a libel suit, but he can get at the paper through the advertisers. However, as a politician and public figure he's in a tight spot—he can't sue for libel because all Denny's doing is challenging his record.''

"Keep trying, Callie. We'll poke around, too.''

Frank hung up the mobile phone. "We have some offices to hit. They're going to be closing soon.''

The state and federal offices were pretty disappointing. "The files on Crowell Chemical and the disaster are pretty thin,'' Frank complained.

"Just as well,'' Joe said as he thumbed through copies. "The gibberish that's here is more than enough for me.''

"They had safety plans,'' Frank said, putting aside a small pile of papers. "And construction permits. But I can't find out what they were storing in the plant at the time of the disaster.

The company's records were lost in the fire. And even these waste permits really don't tell me a lot.''

He tossed the papers from his seat. "There are clues here, hints. I can guess some of the chemicals that might have been there, but that's all it is, pure guesswork. If this is all Denny got, I don't know what kind of a case he'd have. Unless Crowell was storing them illegally. Without proof, though, Denny is never going to convince anyone of his accusations.''

"Maybe there's more at the town office," Joe suggested. "After all, the town people would be the closest to the disaster.''

Frank nodded. "And under Jack Morrison, they were the most crooked.''

"Maybe Crowell isn't as clean as he'd like people to think.''

But when they arrived at the Bayport town hall, they found a small crowd of newspeople gathered outside.

"What's going on here?" Joe asked the group.

"They're waiting for a press statement," a voice from behind them said.

The Hardys turned to find Chet Morton leaning against their van, his hands in his pockets. Their heavyset friend wore a white shirt with the sleeves rolled up and a tie that hung askew from his open collar. He also had a huge grin at their surprised expressions.

"Chet, what are you doing here?" Joe asked. "And why are you dressed like that?"

More to the point, Frank asked, "And how did you know about this press conference?"

"Easy," said Chet, his grin growing. "I work here. The town internship program has me fetching and carrying for Mr. Corrigan, the head clerk."

"So you know all about the files," Frank said.

"First thing I had to learn," Chet agreed. "Mr. Corrigan told me I'd be his arms and legs. But he's a nice guy. That's why I'm out here. He asked me if I wanted a late-afternoon snack."

"Maybe he also wants you to be his stomach," Joe said, patting Chet on the shoulder. "You could make a career out of this."

"Hey, Chet," Frank cut in, "do you think you could get us in to wherever they keep the files on the Crowell Chemical disaster?"

"I suppose I could," Chet said. "If you made it worth my while."

"What's this?" Frank said. "You, almost a public official, asking for a bribe?"

Chet shrugged. "It's the way things get done around here. Mr. Corrigan has a picture up in his office of him and a pal, Howard Zale, down at Zale's retirement home in Florida. The place looks like something from TV—swimming pool, a boat, the works. I guess either Zale never spent a penny he made as fire inspector, or people greased his palm. Now, I was thinking of maybe a pizza . . ."

Joe grinned. "Now, *that's* a way to get a greasy palm."

Laughing, Chet pushed himself away from the van. "Come on, guys. It was worth a try."

He led them around the back of the building and pulled out a key and let them in through a steel door. "Don't make any noise," he whispered as he headed downstairs to the basement. "I don't want to get Corrigan on my case."

They headed along a dimly lit corridor, then turned into a large room. Row after row of metal shelves filled the space, and each shelf was filled with brown cardboard file boxes, coded with mysterious letters and numbers.

"This is some system," Frank muttered as he followed Chet. "I'm surprised it's not computerized though."

"The town keeps talking about it, but they don't like the cost of inputting all the data," Chet explained.

"I'm more impressed at how *you* know where the stuff is," said Joe.

"Oh, it's easier than it looks," Chet said, confidently leading them onward. He stopped at a shelf and pointed. "Right there."

The Hardys followed his finger to three empty spaces in the middle of the shelf.

"You wanted to know where the files were *kept*," Chet said with a grin. "Mr. Corrigan had me pull them this morning. That's what the press conference is about."

Frank and Joe looked at each other. "Well, I'm glad we didn't pay him the pizza first," Joe finally said.

"I guess if we want to hear anything about those files, we'll have to wait in line with the press people," Frank said.

"Sorry, guys," Chet said, heading back toward the door. "You know I'd like to help you out—and Denny, too, of course. I figure this must have something to do with what Denny was saying at the party. But Mr. Corrigan has all the papers in his office—"

He cut off in midsentence as he heard footsteps in the hallway outside.

"I don't like this one little bit," a whining voice complained.

"Corrigan," Chet whispered.

"You liked taking our money well enough," a rougher voice answered. "So did Zale." Frank and Joe looked at each other. They recognized the voice. It belonged to George, the guy who had greeted them at Crowell's mansion.

"That was back when Morrison was running

the show," Corrigan said. "Zale had lots of pull with Jack. Now, though, they could hang us—"

"Don't worry," George said. "You've got the substitute records. Soon, people can look through your records all they like. And all they'll find is that Denny Payson is a liar—or crazy." He laughed. "Just as soon as the real stuff goes through your shredder."

Chapter

6

JOE EASED THE door open, putting his eye to the slit he'd created. George and a mousy-looking guy in baggy pants—Corrigan, obviously—were heading down the corridor. In their arms were three brown cardboard boxes like the ones from the file shelves.

George strolled along with one under each arm. Corrigan staggered under the weight of a single box. Looking over his shoulder in annoyance, George slowed his pace to match Corrigan's.

"They're taking all the files on the Crowell disaster," Chet whispered, peering over Joe's shoulder.

"And they're taking them to the shredding

machine," Frank said. "We've got to stop them. The only question is how?"

Joe grinned. "I've got an idea." He leaned forward, whispering in Chet's ear.

A slow smile spread over Chet's face. "Fine," he said. "I didn't really want to keep this job anyway."

As Frank stared in surprise, Chet opened the door and stepped out into the hallway. "Oh, hi, Mr. Corrigan."

"Oh, ah, Chester." Corrigan's voice sounded flustered. "I thought you were out getting a snack."

"I decided it was too late," Chet said. "Hey, are you carrying that to the shredding room? Let me help you."

"That's all right," Corrigan said nervously.

"No, I ought to help." Chet's voice was loud and cheerful. "After all, I'm supposed to be your arms and legs."

Frank peeked out to see Corrigan and Chet struggling over the box. The head clerk looked over at George. "Ah, why don't you go ahead. I'll be right along," Corrigan said.

George shrugged and headed quickly down the corridor. As soon as he was out of sight, Chet let go of the box. Corrigan staggered backward, sending files flying.

Joe pushed the door open. "Hi, we're collecting for the Bayport scrap paper drive. Is that going to the shredding room?''

Corrigan jumped back. "What? *No!*"

"But you just said this was going to the shredder," Chet said.

"Here, we'll help you pick this stuff up." Joe bent down and grabbed a handful of papers. So did Frank.

"You're sure we can't just take that box off your hands?" Joe insisted.

Corrigan shrank back.

Then came a roar from down the hall. George came charging toward them.

"Gee, your friend seems awfully upset," Joe said, heading for the stairs. "Maybe we should be moving along."

Chet faded back into the file room as Frank and Joe ran for the stairs.

"Wait a second! Give me those papers!" Corrigan dropped his box and began pursuing the Hardys, quickly joined by George, who put his boxes down too.

Frank and Joe threw themselves up the stairs. Behind them they could hear the heavy stomping of George's feet and the rabbity, agitated gasping of Corrigan.

They were halfway up the last flight of stairs, and Joe began to think that he and Frank might just make it.

Then George's hamlike hand closed on his ankle.

Caught off-balance, Joe fell, the papers scattering from his hands. He tried to kick himself free, but he couldn't get the leverage. George's crushing grip was bad enough, but he was twisting Joe's leg so that his free leg was caught under him.

"You!" George called up to Frank. "Hold it!"

Already at the top of the stairs, Frank turned—and froze.

"If you want your brother to keep this leg, you'd better toss those papers down."

Frank stared down at Joe, the papers tight in his grasp. "How do I know you'll let him go?"

"You don't," George said, grinning nastily. "That's the risk you take when you go putting your nose where people don't want it." George twisted Joe's ankle a little more, and Joe grimaced in pain. "Come on, kid. This leg doesn't have much give left in it."

Frank stood, undecided what to do. He was too far away to reach Joe before George really hurt him. He looked from the papers in his hand to his brother. But despite his pain, Joe winked at him encouragingly. His eyes went from the papers to George's face.

Now Frank understood. He slumped his

shoulders in defeat. "All right, you win." He raised the papers and came down a step.

George grinned in triumph, stretching out his left hand. His right hand shifted for a new hold on Joe's leg, preparing for a final, leg-breaking twist.

But Frank came no closer. He sent the papers he was holding straight into George's face.

George flinched involuntarily, and Joe, alert for the chance, twisted free. He scrambled up the stairs, intercepting Frank, who was coming down.

"Come on!" Joe pointed to the door above them.

"But, the papers—" Frank was jerked backward as Joe tugged on him.

"Taken care of," Joe gasped.

Frank joined the retreat, just escaping George's furious lunge.

The Hardys clambered up the stairs and out the door. Joe grabbed Frank's arm, steering him around to the side of the building.

Frank risked a quick look behind from the corner. What he saw set him running even harder. "George and Corrigan are still after us," he said.

"So?" Joe didn't waste any more breath on words.

"George's reaching into his coat," Frank gasped. "I think he's unlimbering that cannon."

He looked over at Joe. "This isn't exactly the way I wanted to find out if he has a laser sight."

"No sweat," Joe said.

They had reached the front of the building by then and still they heard George pounding up behind them. But as they charged into the crowd of newspeople, George fell behind.

And when Frank realized what was happening on the steps, he froze, too.

Chet Morton was standing by the front door, two brown file boxes beside him. He kept tossing papers into the hands of the press and media people, who were going wild.

"Sure, I guess you can have them," Chet said into one microphone. "After all, they were just going to put them through the shredder."

That started up a new commotion among the newspeople.

Frank glared at Joe. "So *this* is why you weren't worried when I threw a handful of papers to George. You could have told me about it."

"I had just enough time to tell Chet." Joe grinned. "Look at him up there. He's really enjoying this circus."

"So are the newspeople. They're eating it up."

Joe nodded. "I just hope the guy from the *Times* is around. Liz Webling would be heartbroken to lose out on a scoop like this."

They could hear one reporter reading a report as she stumbled down the steps. "It's been a long time since I took chemistry," she said. "Some of these things I can't even pronounce. But I recognize enough. These chemicals are highly flammable. I didn't know they were allowed to store this stuff."

Frank and Joe stared at each other. "Results," Frank murmured. "Crowell was probably storing barrels of dangerous waste, and just hoping no one would complain."

"I can hardly wait to see the news tonight," Joe said.

That evening, local television was full of the story about the files. The whole Hardy family saw film clips of Chet Morton distributing files, while explaining that they were all headed for the shredder anyway.

But that wasn't all. People were starting to wonder how much Crowell actually knew about the chemicals. Next followed interviews with a very unhappy Mr. Corrigan. According to the head clerk, the distribution of the records was some sort of prank. The real records, he claimed, were inside the building.

"So, they're still hoping their phony records will convince people," Joe said.

A nervous Corrigan went on. "I believe my assistant was only going along with a joke," he said, stumbling over the words nervously. "But there are certain people in this town who will stop at nothing to blacken the name of civic leaders who only want the best for Bayport."

"He didn't mention Denny, or Lucius Crowell," Frank said.

"I'm just glad he didn't mention you," Fenton Hardy said, frowning at the TV screen.

Frank smiled at his father and shook his head. "Corrigan couldn't have done that. If he mentioned us, we'd be interviewed and tell about George. Then he'd have to explain what he was doing at the town hall. Somehow, I don't think that would help."

But the high point of the evening came when the town prosecutor came on the screen. He announced the formation of a grand jury, saying that enough questions had been raised over the Crowell fire to merit fresh investigation. The grand jury would convene within the next few days and would finish its work before the election.

"Now we're getting somewhere!" Joe grinned enthusiastically.

"The question is, how far will it go?" Fenton Hardy cut in. "I'm not sure that those papers Chet gave out will be considered as real evidence. All they say is that Crowell had hazardous material stored in the plant."

"They're better evidence than they'd have been if they were cut to shreds," Joe said.

Laura Hardy's face wasn't happy. "I just wish you wouldn't take such risks."

"Your mother's right," their aunt Gertrude put in as she entered the room. "The pair of you think you're so clever, but you'll find yourselves in real trouble one of these days."

"Relax, everybody," Joe said. "We did our job. From here on in, it's up to the grand jury and the police."

While he was talking, the phone rang.

"I'll get it," Frank said, heading for the kitchen. "It's probably Callie, calling about the story."

When he picked it up, it wasn't Callie's voice he heard. The cold, angry voice belonged to George.

"That was a cute stunt you pulled today," he said. "But you may regret it. There are worse things for your friend Payson than being called a liar—or crazy."

The voice grew colder. "For instance, there's being dead."

Chapter

7

FRANK SLAMMED THE phone into the receiver. He was seething with frustration. If he'd been on the extension in his father's den or in his own room, he'd have activated a small tape recorder. At least he'd have a record of this threat.

But none of that equipment was in the kitchen. Frank looked around the brightly painted room as if it were something from another planet. Maybe it was. It certainly didn't belong in the same world as that voice whispering threats in his ear.

Joe stepped through the doorway. "I heard you hang up and thought you were raiding the ice cream," he said. "We've got a half gallon of mint chocolate fudge—"

He saw the look on his brother's face and his kidding stopped. "What's up?"

"Threats," Frank said.

Joe shrugged his shoulders. "What haven't we heard before?"

"Nothing like this," Frank said. "The threats were against *Denny,* to get *him* off the case." Frank looked as if he had a bad taste in his mouth. "And I even recognized the voice. It was George."

"George, huh? Calling us to threaten Denny? Did you tell him he had the wrong number?"

Frank shook his head. "The question is, who do we tell about this call? Denny? I don't see him being very impressed."

"How about the cops?" Joe suggested. "Con Riley—or maybe Chief Collig?"

That got another head shake from Frank. "This is a political case. Collig will walk very carefully. And remember the way Con questioned Denny after the shooting at his house? I don't think Denny rates very high on Con's top forty. And I'll bet he won't listen to anything we tell him. He already thinks we're too friendly with Denny."

Joe frowned. "Who else then? How about Barbara—or Denny's mom?"

Frank looked unhappy. "It will just upset them. And I don't think either of them will change Denny's mind."

They both stood in silence. Finally Joe said, "Well, that takes care of the possibilities for talk. How about action?"

He looked at his brother. "What do you say we keep an eye on Denny, just to make sure he doesn't get in any trouble."

Frank nodded with a rueful grin. "I guess it's the best we can do. We've got no proof of what Crowell is up to, and there's no way we can stop Denny. At least we can make sure he doesn't do anything stupid."

"Or that nothing stupid happens to him," Joe added. "Okay. Denny doesn't know it yet, but he's just gained himself a pair of guardian angels."

Joe popped out of the room, heading upstairs. A few minutes later he came back down, carrying a pair of fishing rods.

"What're these for?" Frank asked.

"Oh, this is the great idea you just had a moment ago. We're going fishing tomorrow. I'm going in to tell Mom and Dad. That way they'll know why we're getting up so early in the morning."

With a cheerful grin, Joe headed into the living room.

Frank stared after him wordlessly. "Fishing," he finally said. "Fishing for trouble is more like it. I just hope we don't find too much for Denny to handle."

*   *   *

The next morning dawned beautifully. The sky was clear, and the sun bounced pink light off the few clouds scudding by. A heavy dew covered the tall grass, and the whole world smelled fresh and new.

Frank Hardy sneezed, then picked up his binoculars. "This is stupid," he muttered for the tenth time. "And I'm freezing." He shivered in the dawn chill.

Frank and Joe were standing in the woods at about the same spot the hidden gunman had fired at them. Behind them was their van, pulled off the road and hidden among the trees. They had slogged through grass and weeds, the dew soaking their pants from the knees down. At last they'd found a vantage point where they could watch the Payson house. Every window was still dark.

"I've got half a mind to go down there and wake Denny up." Frank let the binoculars hang around his neck as he rubbed his arms, trying to warm them.

"I know how you feel," Joe said, throwing his arms out and cracking a big yawn. "But I think you might be giving him just a little too much warning. We both agreed last night that he shouldn't know we were around."

"Yeah," Frank said glumly. "So we stand out here cold while he lies in bed."

"Where else could we pick him **up**?" Joe asked. "This is the only place where we know he'll be."

"Right," Frank agreed. "But this is going to get worse before it gets better."

Through the field glasses, they watched Denny and his mom enjoy breakfast—they had a perfect view through the kitchen window. Then Mrs. Payson left for work, and Denny went up to his room. The Hardys watched him work at his desk for a while.

Midmorning came, and Denny switched off the radio, headed downstairs, and got into his car.

"Get ready," Frank said, following Denny with his binoculars.

"I've got a quarter that says he turns left, heading for Bayport," Joe said, fading back to start the van.

"Then you're out twenty-five cents." Frank grinned as he tracked Denny's gray sports car making a right-hand turn onto the county road.

"Well, come on," Joe called as the van roared into life. "We don't want to lose him after all this."

They stayed well behind Denny's car as they started off, not wanting to advertise their presence. They hoped he wouldn't recognize the black van. They had spent some time changing its appearance after they had pulled off into the woods. Carefully applied bands of red and white tape gave the impression of pinstriping on the all-black exterior. And a pair of magnetic signs on the side panels identified the van as a delivery truck for Clover Cleaners.

Joe had even added a touch to partially obscure his face at the steering wheel. A pair of red fuzzy dice dangled from the rearview mirror, and he pulled a baseball cap down to shade his eyes. Frank stayed in the back of the van; a cleaners that sent out a two-man delivery team might be noticed.

Joe moved a bit closer as Denny came to the first big intersection, but the gray car continued straight, farther away from Bayport.

"Where's he going?" Joe asked as they kept driving.

"I've got an idea," Frank said, bracing himself against Joe's seat. "If I'm correct, he'll be making a left soon. You should head over to the right."

They were passing a large industrial park, and sure enough, the gray car's lights flashed, indicating a left turn.

"Okay, pull past him, then turn into the parking lot of this fast-food joint. We can keep an eye on him from across the street there."

Joe coasted to a stop at the end of the lot. Denny's car was still in sight, stopped at the entrance gate. "The mystery is solved," Joe said, as he read the sign by the gate. "So this is the new home of Crowell Chemicals."

"According to the reports, it's one of the safest plants in the country," Frank said.

"Crowell must be awfully proud about it."

"Or awfully guilty about the last one," Frank added.

"Well, it doesn't look as though Denny's going to get a guided tour," Joe said as he watched.

Across the street, the gates were still closed in front of Denny's car. A security man in a brown uniform was shaking his head and pointing at something on his clipboard.

"Guess he's not on the welcome list," Frank said.

Finally Denny gave up arguing and climbed back in his car. He drove toward Bayport again.

"A long drive for a short visit." Joe started the van, watched the traffic, then pulled out smoothly behind Denny's car.

He held the van's speed down, letting Denny take a big lead, which was lucky. From out of another gate in the industrial complex roared a large dark green car, which slid in right behind Denny.

"The plot thickens," said Joe. "You think Denny's got himself another tail?"

"Well, it makes a change from the usual big

black car,'' Frank said, joking. "Let's see what happens.''

The car stayed almost on Denny's rear bumper. When he switched lanes, it pulled in right behind him. When Denny speeded up, so did the green car. When he slowed down, the new shadow didn't take the chance to pass.

"Get over in the fast lane," Frank said. "We'll pass both of them. I want a look at the driver of the green monster."

As Joe sped up, Frank headed to the rear of the van. He stood by the back window, positioning himself so he could see without being seen.

They were just passing the green car, and Frank had a clear view of the driver.

It was George.

"Well, well," said Frank. "It must be the butler's day off."

They passed Denny, and Frank went back up front. Joe was constantly glancing in the rearview mirrors, keeping his targets in sight. "This is the hardest way to tail somebody," he said. "I hope they give us some notice if they decide to turn off."

Frank scanned the road before them. "Get behind that old station wagon ahead there. He's moving slowly enough to let them get past you again."

They drove almost to Bayport, Denny in the lead, Joe drawing near, then dropping back, and

George carefully staying on Denny's tail. Together they got off the county road and drove up to a major intersection. Denny slid to a stop as the traffic light turned red. Then he roared across, running the light.

George never even had a chance to start. The cross traffic cut him off.

And for the Hardys, two cars back, pursuit was impossible.

"I told you we should have a helicopter rig for times like this," Joe said.

"It would make us too noticeable," Frank answered. "Besides, we haven't lost him yet."

"Oh, no?" Joe asked. "Well, that was one of the sweetest imitation escapes I've ever seen."

Frank grinned. "Stop thinking like a detective for a second and think like a real person. This is Clarendon Avenue. Who lives around here?"

The light changed, and Joe shot a look at his brother. "Barbara Lynch."

As George went roaring off in the direction Denny had taken, Frank and Joe headed straight for Barbara's house. A couple of minutes after they took a position on the corner, Denny's car pulled up. Barbara came running from her door, and the chase was on again.

For the rest of the day, the Hardys followed Denny and Barbara all over Bayport as they visited house after house. The same pattern repeated itself at each house. Denny's car would stop outside, Denny and Barbara would go in. A few minutes later they'd come back out, looking unhappy. Denny would make a mark on a piece of paper, and they'd be off again.

Inside the van, Frank was busy noting each address that Denny stopped at. After he'd collected a page full of addresses, he used the mobile phone to dial his father.

"I'm glad you're in, Dad," he said. "Could you use that special directory you've got to put a name to some addresses?"

Fenton Hardy laughed. "I thought that story you gave us sounded pretty fishy," he said. "What's up?"

"We're just keeping an eye on Denny, and I'd like to know who he's meeting." Frank read off a few of the addresses, and his father consulted the directory. The first three names he gave Frank were those of complete strangers, but the fourth rang a bell. "Catherine Gunther—that sounds familiar."

Suddenly he remembered a newspaper page, with the pictures of five men. One of them was Denny's dad. And the caption on another read . . . "George Gunther," Frank said, snapping his fingers. "He was one of the people who died in the Crowell disaster. Thanks a lot, Dad." Frank hung up the phone.

Now Denny's wanderings made sense. "He must be trying to track down anyone who was at the fire," Frank said. "The plant would be the easiest place, but Lucius won't let him talk to anyone who's still working for the company. So Denny's trying ex-employees."

"But why visit Mrs. Gunther?" Joe asked. "He'd know Gunther was dead."

Frank shrugged. "Maybe they had friends who worked there. Who knows? At least we have a handle on what he's doing. He's looking for witnesses."

"And not finding any, from the look on his face," Joe added.

Denny and Barbara were looking very discouraged as they drove into downtown Bayport. They parked the car and then walked into the low-rent district. It was crammed against the commercial area, across the railroad tracks from the neat homes they'd been visiting.

Here they passed shabby frame houses with weed-filled front lawns and sagging porches. Some of the houses had been painted white in an attempt to spruce them up. Others had been painted gray or brown to hide the dirt. On most of them, the paint was peeling.

As Denny and Barbara walked along the cracked pavement, Frank and Joe followed far behind. They were afraid they'd be recognized instantly if Denny and Barbara turned around.

It was getting dark and the streetlights were

just coming on. Frank didn't think they made the neighborhood look better.

Denny apparently agreed. He had stopped and was talking with Barbara, who was shaking her head. Barbara pointed back the way they had come, and Frank and Joe both became suddenly interested in the window display of a hardware store.

"Look," said Joe. "A sale on drills."

"Very funny," Frank answered. "We're going to look really smart when Denny starts walking Barbara back."

They stole a glance and saw that the discussion was getting warmer.

"No, I think Barbara has taken Callie Shaw lessons," Joe said with a grin. "She's going to walk back by herself."

Even as he was saying it, Barbara started walking. Denny reached out to stop her, then shrugged. The Hardys didn't have time for more. They had to get down a side street before Barbara recognized them.

Turning the nearest corner, they walked halfway down the block. Then they turned, waiting for Barbara to pass by. She crossed the street and marched on at top speed, never once looking their way.

Immediately Frank and Joe headed back to the corner. "I hope we don't lose Denny because of this," Joe said.

"*I* hope Denny isn't staring after her and sees us coming around," Frank replied.

But before they reached the corner, they stopped, seeing a familiar bulky figure diagonally opposite from them.

It was George, leaning against a building.

Somehow, he had caught up with Denny and Barbara. But as he stepped away from the building, his eyes weren't trained in the direction Denny had gone.

No, he was looking the other way, the way he started walking a moment later.

After Barbara Lynch.

Chapter

8

JOE STARED AT George for a second, a dangerous light in his eyes. "That guy just made a big mistake."

Once Joe had a girlfriend who had gotten in the way when terrorists were trying to get at the Hardys. The result: an exploding car, and Iola Morton disappearing in a ball of fire. Joe had sworn that he'd never let something like that happen again.

That vow rang in his mind as he dashed for the corner. His face was set, hard and determined.

Both Hardys raced forward and reached the corner together, staring into the gathering darkness.

But Barbara Lynch was nowhere to be seen. Neither was George.

Joe stalked down the street, his legs stiff, his hands balled into fists at his sides. "Go across," he told Frank. "We'll head along this way, checking all the side streets."

Urgency rushed their steps as they ran from corner to corner, checking the darkened side streets. They carefully probed the shadows, alert for anything out of place, straining their ears for a muffled scream or the sounds of a struggle.

They reached the third corner and again their search came up empty. Frank looked around nervously. "What if—"

"No!" Joe cut him off. "They had to come this way. They *had* to!"

He raced to the next corner and turned to look down the side street. Nothing—but wait! His eye caught a movement farther down the street straight ahead. The slight figure of a girl passed a lit window. Seconds later a heavy figure passed also, close behind the girl.

"Come on!" Joe shouted. He and Frank went charging down the street, not caring if the slap of their feet alerted George.

In spite of their lung-bursting pace, they still had a way to go before catching up to the oblivious Barbara and her pursuer. Half a block loomed before them as George reached out and touched Barbara's shoulder.

Both Hardys prepared to attack, speeding up their pace. But George only spoke to Barbara for a moment, then hurried past her.

Barbara herself turned nervously around as she heard rushing footsteps approaching her. Then she recognized her imagined muggers. "Frank! Joe! What's the big idea?" she demanded. "You nearly scared me to death!"

"That guy," Joe gasped. "What did he want with you? What did he say?"

"That man just now?" Barbara said, blinking in surprise. "He just asked for the time and told me I shouldn't be walking alone in this neighborhood."

Frank slammed his hand against an out-of-order streetlight. "Suckered! He suckered us!"

"What do you mean?" Joe said.

But Frank was already heading back down the block. "He must have seen us keeping an eye on Denny, and wanted to draw us off. And what easier way than seeming to threaten Barbara?" he yelled back at them.

"Denny? Denny's in trouble?" Barbara was rushing right beside them.

Frank didn't answer. At the pace he was setting, it was hard enough to breathe. He just hoped they'd catch up with Denny before it was too late.

They hadn't gone very far past the spot where Denny and Barbara had split up when they heard muffled sounds.

"Come on, hold him," a nasal voice commanded. Then came grunting and the unmistakable sound of a punch.

"There's a phone over there," Frank said to Barbara, pointing to the corner. "Call the cops."

He and Joe headed for the mouth of the alley where all the noise came from. Torn bags of uncollected garbage piled up at the entrance. Just beyond them, two guys were working Denny over.

The owner of the nasal voice was a tall punk with acne. He threw a punch into Denny, giving him a big grin as he drew his fist back again. His partner was big and heavy, hanging on as Denny struggled to get free.

Denny's cheek was swollen, and a thin trail of blood dribbled down his chin from a split lip. The moose had no trouble hauling him around for his grinning partner's next punch.

"You go after the moose," Joe whispered. "I'll take care of Smiley."

Frank nodded soundlessly, and they both stepped into the alley.

Coming up behind the guy holding Denny, Frank set his hands deep into his blubbery neck and whipped the guy toward a wall. Denny fought free just as his captor crashed into brick.

"Hey!" yelled the puncher. But even as he was speaking, he felt a tap on his shoulder. He turned—to see Joe Hardy's fist flying at his face.

Both guys were surprised, but they didn't give up the fight. Big Boy shambled back from the wall, throwing a roundhouse right at Frank. His partner faked a punch at Joe, then kicked his knee.

Frank grabbed the arm in the middle of its clumsy punch and twisted. Big Boy bellowed in pain, tearing his arm out of Frank's grasp. Joe sidestepped Smiley's leg and landed a fist in his belly. The skinny punk folded, staggering backward toward the end of the alley.

Suddenly he straightened up, his teeth gritted in pain as he hurled a bag of garbage at the Hardys. The bag was half-torn, and it showered Frank, Joe, and Denny in glop.

The two guys took that moment to run off. A siren howled nearby, and seconds later two police officers stood at the alley entrance, hands on the butts of their pistols. "All right," one called. "What's going on in there?"

"Two guys attacked our friend," Joe said, pointing at Denny, who was leaning against a wall as Barbara dabbed at his lip with a tissue. "They ran when they heard you coming."

A flashlight beam cut through the darkness,

to rest on the four of them. "Attacked you with garbage, it looks like," one of the cops said. "Unless you boys play funny."

"We'll hear all about it," said his partner. "At the station."

The back seat of the patrol car had a sour smell, part disinfectant, part unwashed bodies. It probably wasn't the first time someone reeking of garbage had sat back there.

"At least they saw Barbara back to my car," Denny said. "Lucky she has an extra set of keys."

"Yeah," Frank agreed, staring at the cagework that set them off from the front seat, and the doors with no handles. "Real lucky."

Early the next morning Frank stepped out of the shower, his fourth since the evening before, and cautiously sniffed the air. At least he didn't smell like a walking landfill anymore. His father had looked torn between yelling or laughing at them when he saw their bedraggled appearance the night before.

"Well," Fenton Hardy had said as he went to pick them up, "at least you had some consideration. If I have to show up at the police station, I'd prefer to go early in the evening, rather than at two A.M. Just do me a favor on the way home. Keep all the windows down."

As he walked down the stairs, Frank thought

that neither his mother nor his father was very happy about their adventure. Sure, he and Joe had saved Denny Payson. But they hadn't done a great job of protecting him.

Frank walked into the kitchen, where Joe was halfheartedly dipping a spoon into a bowl of cereal.

"Not hungry?"

Joe shook his head. "Every time I take a bite, I smell last night," he said.

Frank's hand went to his stomach. "Thanks."

He poured himself a glass of orange juice and sat at the table.

"You know," said Joe, "we need a new plan. As long as Crowell and George are around, Denny's in danger. They can get to him. Last night proves that. So what are we going to do?"

"Talk to Denny," Frank answered promptly. "Then get to work cracking this case open."

"Well, we'll get a chance at step one pretty soon," Joe said, looking out the window. "Here comes Denny now."

They opened the back door before Denny even knocked. He had a newspaper crumpled in one hand, and his face was white with rage. The swelling on his cheek had gone down and was now a livid bruise, and his lip was still puffy and cut. "I thought *you guys* were helping me, until I saw this."

Unfolding the paper, he held up the front

page. "Payson in Alley Scuffle," the headline read. Under it was a photo, obviously shot by a reporter who happened to be at the police station. Frank remembered the camera flash. It showed a wild-eyed Denny being hustled up the station house steps. The photo had been cropped to cut the Hardys out.

"You're not in the picture, and you're not in the story either." Denny's finger stabbed at the columns of type beside the photo.

Frank zipped through the story, growing angrier with each line he read. "During the day Payson caused a scene at the Crowell Chemical Plant. . . . upset a number of ex-Crowell employees with wild accusations . . . ended in a fight in the worst section of town . . . Unstable since losing his father five years ago . . . Neighbors describe him as 'troubled.' "

" 'Troubled'!" Denny shouted, crumpling the paper again. "They're trying to make me out as some kind of crazy to discredit what I'm saying about Crowell."

"Somebody's certainly managing the news," Frank agreed grimly.

"That wasn't the *Times*, was it?" Joe asked.

"No, it's the *Courant*," Frank answered. "They eat up the spicier news."

"Let me see that." Joe reached out for the paper.

Frank turned to Denny, who was pacing up

and down. "You know who's behind all this—" he began.

Then the phone rang. When Frank answered it, he stared in amazement. "Speak of the devil," he said.

"This is Lucius Crowell." The agitated voice was unmistakable. "I called the Paysons and heard that Denny was coming over there. Please. I've got to speak to him. I was very upset to learn what happened last night."

"What are you going to tell us, the right hand doesn't know who the left hand is punching?" Frank asked. "Don't try to kid me. I was there last night. Your man George set it up."

"He's not my man," Crowell said angrily. "He's in charge of security for the plant, and for me personally."

"Well, you'll be glad to hear that he loves his job."

Crowell sighed, but he wasn't about to say anything on a line that might connect to a tape recorder. "I've got to talk to Denny. No matter what mistakes I may have made in the past, I've got to make him understand. He's setting himself up as a target—and I'm afraid for him. He'll get himself hurt."

This wasn't a threat. Nor was it the bogus "sincerity" of one of Crowell's campaign speeches. It was pleading from a man who sounded genuinely fond of Denny, and worried for him.

Frank was a little surprised to hear himself saying, "Let me see if he'll come to the phone."

He turned to Denny. "It's Crowell. He wants to talk with you."

Denny stared at the phone as if Frank were handing him a rattlesnake. Then he turned on his heel and headed for the door.

His face was cold as ice when he turned back in the doorway.

"Tell him, sure, I'll talk to him—as soon as he brings my father back!"

Chapter

9

AFTER DENNY PAYSON stormed off, the Hardys tried to get a new handle on the case. "We know that Crowell did something wrong, which resulted in the disaster at the chemical plant." Frank leaned his elbows on the kitchen table. "The question is, how do we prove it?"

"Not easy," Joe had to say. "Especially with Crowell's lawyers trying to block the use of those files we found. What else do we know?"

They went over and over what they had found out so far. "Wait a second," Joe finally said. "Remember when Chet took us down to the town records?"

Frank nodded.

"Remember, he mentioned a picture that Corrigan kept in his office. Corrigan visiting his rich friend at his ritzy house in Florida.''

"Zale." Frank frowned as he dug up the name. "Howard Zale."

"Right!" Joe exclaimed. "He was the fire inspector. Chet thought he had taken money."

"We *know* he was taking money," Frank cut in. "George said as much when they were taking those papers to be shredded."

Joe nodded. "You're right. It just slipped by me in all the excitement."

"Well, we remembered now." Frank pushed himself away from the table. "Let's see what kind of story we can get on Howard Zale. I wonder if he had anything to do with the fire."

He led the way upstairs to his room, pulled the dust cover off his computer, and started attaching his modem unit to the phone. In moments, he was plugging into local information networks.

"The town data base lists him as a fire and safety inspector. I'll bet that he was in charge of the investigation of the fire. And as the safety inspector he probably knew that Crowell was violating safety regulations." Frank hit some buttons as he read from his screen, and the computer printer began to rattle as it printed out the information. "Hmmmm. Retired very recently. Shortly after Jack Morrison was murdered."

"Maybe he got cold feet," Joe suggested. "Now that he wouldn't have his buddy around to take care of him."

But Frank was barely listening, working hard at the keyboard. "There are no Zales listed as living in Bayport," he said, wiping out the screen. "No family members to help us track him down."

He frowned for a second, then reached for a box of floppy disks. "One of my hacker friends got some access codes we might use—"

Popping a disk into the computer, he bent over the keyboard. New writing appeared on the screen.

"What's this?" Joe asked, leaning forward to get a look.

"The town's pension list. If Zale is retired, he's probably getting a pension."

They quickly ran to the end of the list, but there was no Zale to be found.

"This is weird," Joe complained. "From what we know about him, Zale was picking up money wherever he found it. I can't believe he'd give up on his own pension."

"I know of one reason." Frank's face was grim as he hit more computer keys. A new list appeared on the screen, and he quickly rolled to the end of it.

"There he is!" Joe pointed. "Howard Zale! We found him!"

"Yeah," Frank said flatly. "On the list of deceased town workers." He hit some more keys, then read something off the screen. "Died of a heart attack, about six weeks ago. Long before anyone started digging into the case."

"We spend all this time finding one good lead, and he's dead and buried." Joe sighed.

Frank turned off the computer and disconnected the modem. Just as he was putting the cover back on, the telephone rang.

He picked up the phone. "Hi, Mrs. Payson. No, Denny's not here. He left a while ago." Suddenly Frank was leaning forward in his chair. "What? He hasn't shown up? Okay, Mrs. Payson. We'll take a look around."

Hanging up the phone, he turned to Joe. "The grand jury hearing starts in about an hour, and Denny was supposed to go with his mother. He hasn't shown up at home."

Joe immediately headed out of the room. "Let's find out if anybody's seen him."

Getting in the van, they searched the usual hangouts in town, but no one had noticed Denny Payson.

At the Mr. Pizza in the mall, Liz Webling blocked their way out the door. She'd left her slice on the counter and pulled out a pad when she heard the Hardys questioning people.

"Do you think he's disappeared?" she asked

them. "Could this have something to do with that fight last night?"

"Liz, give us a break," Joe said. "This is a *friend* we're talking about."

"Hey, Liz," said Callie Shaw, joining the group, "isn't that your slice Chet's picking up?"

Liz turned, and the Hardys and Callie beat a hasty retreat. "She's going to be a long time forgiving me for that," Callie said. "What's going on?"

Frank quickly explained as they headed back to the van.

Callie thought for a moment. "Have you talked to Barbara Lynch?"

"Good idea," said Joe, veering off to a set of pay phones.

They were lucky. Barbara was home. But she hadn't seen Denny all day. "The last I saw him was when I drove his car to his house last night," she said.

"We talked for a little bit then. He was pretty depressed. Here we'd spent the whole day tracking down people from this list he'd made of potential witnesses for the grand jury and nobody'd come forward. Denny had only one name left, a man who lived in that run-down neighborhood."

"Wait a second," said Frank after Joe passed on this message. "He never made it to that person. He got ambushed. Ask Barbara if she remembers the address.''

Joe asked, then shook his head. "She says it wasn't even on his list. He'd gotten it from the widow of one of the workers who died.''

Frank thought for a moment. "Mrs. Gunther?''

Joe nodded.

"Thank her and then let's go. I've got Mrs. Gunther's address in the van.''

They drove up to Mrs. Gunther's. Frank jumped out of the van and headed up the path to the front door.

At the first ring of the bell, a gray-haired woman appeared. She looked at him warily through the screen door.

"Mrs. Gunther?" Frank said. "I'm Frank Hardy, a friend of Denny Payson's. Denny's mother needs him and I think he's at the address you gave him yesterday. I hate to bother you, but it's very important.''

"I sent him to see a man who was a friend of my husband's," Mrs. Gunther said. "Steve Vittorio." She gave Frank the address. It was just beyond where the two punks had jumped Denny.

"Thanks, ma'am," Frank said, already hurrying back to the van. "Thanks very much.''

The neighborhood looked less threatening in broad daylight, but shabbier than ever.

"Twenty-nine South Bay," Frank said, pointing to an old apartment building. "That must be the place."

Leaving Callie to guard the van, Frank and Joe entered the building. Half the mailboxes had broken doors. None of them had names.

Joe pointed to a sign taped to the wall. "Apartment available," he read. "Inquire at apartment One-A." He grinned. "Maybe we could inquire about Vittorio there."

They knocked at apartment 1-A, and the door opened to reveal a tall, skinny man in a coverall that looked about two sizes too large for him. He scratched the stubble of beard on his chin as he squinted at the Hardys. "You here to see the apartment?" he asked.

"We're here to see Steve Vittorio," Joe said.

"Well, you can't," said the janitor. "He moved out, and he didn't leave anything. What's your problem? He owe you money?"

"We're not bill collectors," Frank said. "A friend of ours was looking for Vittorio, and we thought we'd catch up with him here."

"Skinny kid with red hair?" asked the custodian. "He was here early this morning. But Steve ain't been here for months. He was living here after he quit at that big chemical plant—"

"Crowell?" Joe asked.

The man nodded. "And he finally got a shot

at a decent job in Philly. Foreman on a building project.''

"Philadelphia?" said Frank.

"That's what I said." The man shook his head. "Never seen a guy get so popular so long after he moved away. You're the third guys to come asking for him today."

Joe stared at the janitor. "Somebody else came asking about Vittorio?"

"Yeah. Big bruiser. Mean looking. I thought he was a bill collector, for sure."

"Balding guy?" Frank asked. "Scar on his cheek?"

"That's him." The custodian shivered. "He got pretty mad when I couldn't tell him where Steve was living in Philly." He shrugged. "People from here don't usually leave a forwarding address."

"When did this second guy show up?" Joe asked.

The man shrugged again. "It was a while after the kid left. I don't really know."

"Well, thanks for your help," Frank said, grabbing Joe's arm and heading out of the building.

"What do we do now?" Joe wanted to know.

"Get into the van and get moving," Frank answered.

They reached the van and brought Callie up to date. "I suspect Denny is heading for Philadelphia," Frank said as he finished his story. "The problem is, so is George. We've got to check it out."

"Can't the police—" Callie began.

"What can the cops do?" Joe asked. "Neither of them is suspected of a crime—yet."

"But he threatened you guys and shot at you," Callie insisted.

"Proof—we don't have any, and it's our word against his," Joe answered.

"We need you to organize things on this end," Frank said. "Keep on the lookout for Denny. And maybe you and Barbara can make sure Mrs. Payson gets to the opening of the grand jury."

"*Real* exciting," Callie said. Then she shrugged. "But necessary, I guess. I hope you guys catch up with Denny."

"Before George does," Joe muttered.

The drive to Philadelphia took a couple of hours. All the way the Hardys' stomachs reminded them that they were missing lunch. Finally, near the Pennsylvania border, Frank pulled the van over at a truck stop.

"Get some burgers and something to drink for both of us," he told Joe.

"What are you going to do?" Joe asked.

Frank got out his lap-top computer and modem, and pointed to a nearby pay phone. "I'm going to talk to a few data bases to see if I can find out anything about a new foreman named Vittorio." He grinned. "We may be running behind in the race, but we might be the first ones to reach the finish. Find Vittorio, and sooner or later, Denny and George will appear."

By the time Joe came back with the food, Frank was stowing away his computer with a satisfied smile. "I think I have our man. A Stephen Vittorio recently was hired as foreman for a construction project on Market Street." He showed Joe the address. "We should be able to catch him on the job. They won't have knocked off yet."

Traffic was heavy as they drove through the Philadelphia streets. It slowed the Hardys down, and they had a terrible time finding a parking spot. At last, however, they were walking toward the construction site.

It was easy enough to find. A huge crane in the middle of the block made a hard-to-miss landmark. The crane's engine roared into life, and a pallet of cinder blocks and sacks of concrete started rising to an upper floor. At the foot of the crane, a man in a hard hat wrote something on a clipboard.

"Looks as though that guy is in charge around here," Joe said. "Maybe he can steer us in Vittorio's direction."

Since the sidewalk was blocked off, they had

to step into the street to get to the man. He looked up from his clipboard as a guy on the second floor of the unfinished building shouted down to him.

"Hey, Steve," the construction worker yelled, "we need some sweepers up here."

Frank looked at Joe. "Steve! Maybe he's the guy we're looking for."

The Hardys quickened their pace. Just as they reached the rear of the crane, they saw someone approaching from the opposite direction. Denny Payson!

His eyes were fixed on Steve Vittorio as he hurried up.

"Well, Denny found him," Frank said.

"I just hope George didn't," Joe muttered.

As if in answer to Joe's comment, a flash of red light came from across the street.

"Denny! Duck!" Frank and Joe both yelled.

Even as they hit the dirt, they realized that the laser, and the two shots that followed, were aimed high over their heads.

They looked up to see the crane's load start to tilt. The shots had been aimed at the metal cable holding the pallet.

With a metallic *twang*, the strands parted— and a ton of concrete blocks fell toward them!

Chapter
10

DENNY PAYSON THREW himself backward. So did Frank and Joe. But the man with least warning was Steve Vittorio. He had barely started moving as the concrete came whistling down.

Denny's voice was a shriek. "You miserable, murdering—"

His words were drowned out by the roar of concrete hitting the street. The cinder blocks came down like an urban landslide. Some smashed onto the covered walkway, turning its wooden roof into toothpicks. Other loose blocks crashed into the crane itself, making the whole structure quiver. But most of the blocks came cascading down right in front of the Hardys.

Frank and Joe hugged the ground. They

coughed in the gritty cloud of concrete dust that mercifully blotted out the scene.

As the choking cloud settled, they could see a figure rising in the distance. For a wild second, Joe thought he was seeing a ghost. It looked like Denny, but the face and clothes were all white. Then he realized that he was covered with dust and noticed that he and Frank were just as badly covered.

"Denny!" Yelling the name tore at Joe's grit-clogged throat.

But Denny was paying no attention to him. He stared wide-eyed and silent at the spot where Steve Vittorio had stood. It looked as if a giant child had dumped all his blocks in one untidy pile after playtime. But there was nothing play-ful about what lay buried there.

Even though they knew it was hopeless, Frank and Joe started pulling the blocks aside, raising another cloud of dust. Joe turned, ex-pecting to see Denny run to help. Instead, he saw his friend tearing like a madman down the street.

But the construction workers were joining in, shifting the blocks away. Joe stepped back, coughing from the dust. And when he looked up again, he was staring at a heavyset guy helping to clear the debris—he was paying special atten-tion to the concrete bags. Joe couldn't believe it. George!

Joe nudged Frank. "Look. First he kills Vittorio, then he joins the rescuers. We've got to get the police."

Frank stared at George. "No. We will—in a minute." Frank watched him a little longer. "He's searching for something." His eyes narrowed. "There were two shots. Suppose one missed the cable altogether and wound up in one of those concrete sacks? A spent bullet could be checked by the police ballistics lab. It would be proof that he killed Steve Vittorio."

He looked eagerly at Joe. "We've got to stop him from finding that bullet. But how?"

A slow smile spread over Joe's face. "I'll show you. Just follow my lead."

Joe headed across the wreckage, to an area George hadn't searched yet. Several bags of concrete lay around. Miraculously some had held together. Others had spread their contents across the street. Joe stooped over and began poking through them.

Then he yelled, "Hey, George!"

The big guy looked up, startled, just in time to see Joe snatch something up from the ground. He pocketed it and smiled. "Too late. I've got your little souvenir."

George's hand went under his coat. Then he hesitated, glancing around at all the people around him.

Joe took off running, right into the construction site, with Frank on his heels. They turned for an instant to see George hurrying after them.

All work had stopped on the site as the workers swarmed to try to rescue Vittorio. The Hardys dashed past a row of concrete pillars, then took a sharp right, hiding behind a rough cinder-block wall.

"You're sure it was a good idea to leave the safety of the crowd?" Frank asked.

"We'll lose him in here, then we have to get the cops," Joe said. "I don't think those hard-hats would believe us if we started telling them about shots and lasers."

The sound of pounding footsteps behind them made the Hardys push off and start to run again. "Come on. He won't be able to keep up with us," Joe said, breathing hard.

But somehow, George did stay with them. He didn't draw close enough to risk a shot, but he had the long-barreled pistol with the boxy laser sight mounted on top in his hand.

"We can't get past that machinery. Let's go over," Joe whispered, pointing to a flight of stairs in the center of the unfinished building. They started up silently, but soon the clang of bare metal gave them away. George came charging after them.

They started to jump off on the open side of the stairs, then saw the red flash of the laser sight. If they got off, George would have a clear shot at them.

"Didn't think about that," Joe admitted as they pushed themselves up another flight.

The building was less and less finished the farther up they went. The next floor they reached had hardly any walls at all, just vast open spaces. It would be a killing ground if George caught up with them.

"We're running out of hiding places," Joe gasped.

"And stairs," Frank said grimly, looking up. The only other stairs were on the far side of the building. On every floor they'd passed, an empty oil drum had been left for use as a garbage can. Luckily, one was on this floor as well.

In wordless agreement, the Hardys raced to the drum, turned it on its side, and sent it rolling down the stairs.

They heard George yell as it came bouncing down, but they knew they had won only a brief delay.

Chest burning, Joe tore across the wide expanse of concrete, Frank right at his side. Behind them, they could hear George mounting the stairs again. They'd never reach the stairs on the far side of the building.

Then Frank was grabbing Joe's arm, pulling him off course. He led him to a set of large square holes in the floor, set in the middle of the building. Without letting go of Joe, Frank threw himself over the edge.

As they dropped, a gunshot rang out over their heads.

Joe closed his eyes—and suddenly found himself stopping, then bouncing in the air.

His eyes popped open. He was on a net, which was springing up and down like a trampoline.

Frank was already on his knees, pulling Joe to the safety of the floor.

"What?" Joe said as he and his brother started moving again.

"Elevator shafts," Frank explained, pointing to the hole above them. "They just haven't put the elevators in yet. The safety rules say that nets have to be strung across the open shafts every few floors. I figured there had to be at least one net between us and the ground."

He pushed Joe back to the stairs. "Now come on, before George decides to drop in on us."

They dashed across the floor, Joe still shaking his head. "He thinks there'll *probably* be a net between us and the ground. And people think *I'm* the crazy one in this team."

Taking the steps two at a time, they raced down the final flight of stairs. Soon they were back on the first floor.

"Which way to the van?" Frank asked. "All this running has left me turned around."

"This way." Joe pointed. "I remember passing those big metal boxes."

Frank broke into a jog, quickly retracing their path. "We've lost him for now, but we have no idea when he might turn up again."

They reached the edge of the site, which was now crammed with workers. Mingling with the crowd, they worked their way out to the street.

"You know," Joe said to Frank, "we can cut right through that building across the way."

"The warehouse?" Frank said.

"Yeah. We're parked right on the other side. And anything that will save us a few steps . . ."

"Fine," Frank agreed. "We get in the van, get out of here, then find a pay phone." He smiled grimly at his brother's puzzled expression. "We still have to tell the Philadelphia police to search for a bullet. I think an anonymous call might be better than walking up to one of the cops at the site."

Joe grinned. "I guess we might have a hard time convincing a cop to take us seriously." Frank's face was still white with concrete dust, except where running sweat had carved little streaks.

He shrugged. "Well, come on."

They crossed the street, working their way to the rear of the rapidly gathering crowd. Apparently the workers who'd been lounging in front of the warehouse had either joined the rescuers or were part of the crowd. The Hardys had no problem moving past the open double doors of the warehouse.

The first floor was huge and cavernous. It reminded Joe of an enlarged, dingier version of the Bayport records room. Bays of shelving stretched twelve feet up to the ceiling, and they were crammed with a jumbled assortment of packing crates and cardboard boxes. Some of the boxes were broken open, displaying all sorts of paper goods. They even passed a collection of crushed party hats.

Ahead of them was another set of double doors, also standing ajar. Joe could understand why. The air inside the warehouse was musty, stagnant, and hot. Any breeze would be welcome.

Joe ran the back of his sleeve across his eyes, trying to wipe away some sweat. It would be good to get into the van. It had air conditioning, and each of them had a change of clothes stowed in a secret compartment under the floorboards.

He was stepping forward eagerly as they reached the doorway. Then he stopped sharply.

A large green car was drawn up in front of the door.

And sitting in it, his pistol aimed straight at the brothers, was George.

Chapter

11

THE WIDE CENTRAL aisle of the warehouse stretched behind Frank and Joe. They knew that running down that open space would only earn them bullets in their backs.

So, as George got out of his car and rushed the door, Frank darted right, and Joe left.

Joe sighed as he heard heavy footfalls come after him. *Just my luck. Godzilla picks on me again. How did he know where to find us anyway?*

He ducked around several racks of shelves, zigzagging to make sure George couldn't get a clear shot. The strategy seemed to be working, until Joe reached an aisle that was blocked by a forklift truck.

He had to backtrack. He crept along a line of

shelves, straining his eyes and ears for any sight of George. Maybe this could work out. If he could get behind George, he'd be able to sneak out the exit he'd originally been aiming for. Then he could get the cops and nail the killer.

But it didn't turn out exactly as he had planned. He was behind George, but George knew exactly where he was.

Joe's first warning came when he heard the *snick* of a revolver being cocked behind him. He rolled across the floor as the laser's red aiming beam flashed past his face. There was no explosion of gunfire though. George was saving his bullets for a clear shot.

Rising to his knees, Joe scuttled backward behind the shelter of a storage bay. He retreated across one aisle, heading toward the wall of the warehouse. Maybe he could sneak past George this way. He crept to the side of another bay, preparing to leap across the narrow alley to a third set of shelves.

Joe peeked around the corner—and found George waiting for him. Again, the laser flashed past his face, and Joe retreated. He decided to work his way toward the central aisle and slip past George that way.

But when he tried to go down another alley, George was there again, flashing his laser. Joe retreated once more.

Every time he tried to make a break for it, he

encountered an aisle patrolled by George. Slowly he realized what was happening. George was positioning himself at the corners of bays, where he could check down two aisles at once. He was using the beam of his laser to block Joe's escape and herd him backward into a corner of the building. Once he had moved Joe back far enough, he would have no cover. . . .

Joe didn't want to think about it. He had to figure out a way to get past George. Maybe if he showed himself, then stayed in place . . .

He poked his head out, then pulled it back as the familiar red flash came again. Joe counted to ten, giving George enough time to move. He peeked around again, and found that George had indeed moved—closer to him.

The red laser flash was accompanied by a bullet this time. Joe pulled back into a zigzagging retreat again. George's laughter followed him.

Of course. George would orient on the last point where he'd seen Joe. He'd walk down that alley, since Joe couldn't cross it, checking out the cross alleys so Joe couldn't sneak around. No matter which way Joe tried to go, he'd be cut off from the doors. With George moving in, whichever way Joe went, he would soon end up in a corner.

It reminded Joe of chess games he'd had with Frank, where he'd be reduced to moving his lone king around the board as Frank's pieces closed in. With every move, there were fewer and fewer safe squares. . . .

He'd never been able to come out of those games a winner. But this was real. There had to be some way to break out of his box.

Joe looked up at the wall of the warehouse. It had an arrow pointing up, with a sign saying *Stairs*. He started running for it.

If he could reach the stairs, he'd break free of the game board. George would have to search in three dimensions. If he could just make it upstairs . . .

There were only six steps to go when he heard the voice behind him saying, "Nice try, kid."

Slowly Joe turned around. George stood at the bottom of the stairs, his pistol out and ready. It was a chrome-plated revolver, and its barrel looked long enough to reach out and touch Joe on the chest.

"Let's have it," George said.

Joe stared at him. "Have what?"

"Look, don't play cute with me. I want the bullet you picked up."

Now Joe remembered why George was chasing him. He thought Joe was carrying the bullet that would link him to Vittorio's murder!

"I don't have it," Joe said.

The gun was aimed straight at Joe's chest,

and George clicked back the hammer. "I saw you pick it up, kid. Don't try to con me."

"I *pretended* to pick it up, to scare you off," Joe admitted. "Then we were going to call the cops. My brother's probably doing that right now."

George cocked an ear and grinned. "I don't hear any sirens, do you? Maybe your brother messed up." His face went cold again. "Start emptying your pockets."

Joe slowly obeyed, even though he knew it would only buy him a little more time. And time for what?

As Joe began turning his pockets out, Frank Hardy sat watching the scene perched on top of the nearest set of shelves. He was just leaving the warehouse office when he had heard a gunshot and hurried to help his brother.

He hadn't found anything to help them in the office. It contained a desk, lots of papers, a pack of cigarettes and some matches, and an old-fashioned dial phone. The workmen must have been using the phone too much, because there was a lock on it. Frank couldn't even call the police.

He'd snatched up the matches on his way out of the office, however. The hazy beginnings of an idea were forming in his brain.

Now, as he watched Joe in George's line of fire, the idea was his only hope. He had to find some way to neutralize George's gun and laser sight. And his only weapons were the matches and the boxes of paper goods.

While Joe emptied his left-hand pocket, Frank cautiously tore open the carton nearest to him. Loose papers—perfect. He found another box, opened it, then slid the two boxes to the edge of the shelf.

By now, Joe stood with all his pockets turned out, his belongings in his hands. Frank tore out half the matches in the matchbook and lit the boxes of paper. They went up in flames right away.

He shoved them off the shelf and they landed right in front of George.

"Joe! Jump!" Frank yelled. Joe vaulted over the side of the stairs as George shied back from the flames. And even as he was yelling, Frank was striking the rest of his matches and holding them up to a nozzle over his head, part of the warehouse sprinkler system.

Water started spurting down, like an indoor monsoon. It hit the burning paper, sending up a dense cloud of smoke. George coughed and waved a hand in front of his face. The red laser beam stabbed out, but couldn't penetrate the murk.

That was all Frank needed to see. He climbed down off his shelf and took off after his brother.

Frank and Joe stumbled out of the warehouse,

soaking wet. "Well, at least it washed off that concrete dust," Joe said as they ran for their van.

"Just be glad I was carrying the keys. I was afraid you were going to give them to George," Frank shot back as he unlocked the van door.

They were pulling around the corner when George appeared at the warehouse entrance. In the rearview mirror, Frank saw him shove the gun under his jacket and stare after them.

The ride back to Bayport was as fast as legally possible. They stopped once, long enough for Frank to make his warning call to the Philadelphia police. While he was doing that, Joe had changed into dry clothes. Frank changed in the back of the van while Joe drove.

As they reached the outskirts of Bayport, Joe turned onto the road that led to the Paysons' house.

"What's up?" Frank looked at his brother in surprise. "I thought we were going straight to the grand jury hearings."

"I wanted to see if I could catch Denny at home first," Joe said. "When he took off the way he did, I knew he was upset. It's understandable, seeing what happened to Steve Vittorio. But he was Denny's last hope for a witness. I wanted to tell him it's not all over. We have a chance of nailing Crowell through George."

"*If* the Philadelphia police find that spent bullet," Frank reminded him.

"Well, it's better than giving up completely— which, I'm afraid, is what Denny's going to do," Joe answered.

He pulled up in front of the house, and walked up to the front door. "Hey, Denny!" he called, ringing the bell.

The door opened, but it wasn't Denny who greeted him. It was a very pale Mrs. Payson.

"I'm sorry," Joe said. "I thought you'd be in town for the grand jury."

"Barbara and Callie wanted to take me, but I thought I should wait for Denny," Mrs. Payson said. Lines of strain showed on her face as she spoke.

Joe's stomach knotted as he looked at her. "Didn't Denny come back?" he asked.

Mrs. Payson nodded jerkily, trying to hold back tears. "He came back, yes. He pushed by me, went up to his room, then down to the cellar, then out the door and into his car. All without a word. As if I were invisible."

Joe frowned. He didn't like what he was hearing. Waving for Frank to join them, he turned to Mrs. Payson again. "Was he carrying anything?"

"He took something downstairs with him, but I couldn't see what it was." Now tears were forming in Mrs. Payson's eyes. "He had it wrapped up in a coat. I couldn't see."

"I think we'd better go up to Denny's room," Frank suggested quietly. "Maybe we can figure out what it was that Denny took."

They reached the top of the stairs, and turned into Denny's bedroom. Sitting on his desk was the answer to their question.

Joe sighed. He'd been wrong. Denny wasn't about to give up his war against Lucius Crowell.

On his desk was the presentation case for his new gun.

But the gun and the laser sight were both missing.

Chapter

12

FRANK HARDY TURNED to Mrs. Payson, who stood white-faced in the doorway. "Do you know where he went?" he asked.

"After Lucius Crowell," Mrs. Payson whispered. She was obviously on the edge of falling to pieces.

"He won't catch him," Frank said quickly. "I called my dad. The grand jury is still hearing testimony. They'll be in session until about six. And no matter how angry or desperate Denny might be, I can't see him walking into the courtroom to shoot Crowell."

He immediately regretted his words when he saw the look on Mrs. Payson's face.

"Mrs. Payson," Frank said gently, "we don't want Denny to do anything stupid, or have anything stupid happen to him. But if we're going to head him off, we've got to find him as soon as possible."

"Where do you think he might have gone?" Joe asked.

"I—I just don't know," Mrs. Payson said. She looked up hopefully. "Maybe he went over to Barbara's?"

Frank shook his head; he had called on the car phone. Barbara wasn't there, and neither was Denny.

"I'm afraid not, Mrs. Payson," he said.

"Please," Joe asked desperately, *"think,* Mrs. Payson. Is there anyplace Denny goes when he wants to think? When he wants to be alone? Maybe when he was younger?"

Mrs. Payson shook her head. "I really can't— Wait a second."

Frank and Joe turned to her.

"After the fire, Denny used to go to the old Crowell plant. I didn't like the idea, but he was stubborn. Even though I punished him, he refused to stop. He'd ride his bike over there, and just sit, looking at the ruins."

"Nobody's built there, have they?" Frank asked.

"Nope," Joe replied.

They stared at each other. "Let's go check it out," Frank said, heading out of the house and toward the van.

"Might as well," Joe said, following his brother.

Frank started up the van, heading for Shore Road. The old Crowell plant had been on Barmet Bay. Back when the plant had been built, it had probably been the perfect place for dumping. Any chemicals they didn't want, they'd just pour into the bay.

Times had changed though. There were laws against dumping now. Frank remembered reading the federal reports about the new Crowell plant. It had an excellent reputation for the treatment and disposal of waste chemicals. But what about the old plant? What had been kept there?

Joe kept talking as they drove along. "You know, it's funny. Denny never could convince the police that Crowell and George were after him. But if we told the cops that Denny was out with his gun, you'd better believe they'd be scrambling all over town to find *him*."

"I hope we don't have to go that far," Frank said.

Joe's lips twisted. "If we tell the cops, Crowell wins."

"If we don't tell them, Crowell's dead," Frank said.

"This whole case stinks," Joe complained. "We've known who the bad guys were almost from the beginning, but we still can't prove a thing about them."

"And because of that, we've got a friend out there somewhere with a gun. With no one believing him, he may be desperate enough to use it." Frank pounded his fist against the steering wheel. "We've got to find him, Joe."

They came to the road for the old Crowell plant. Frank turned the van, and they started jouncing along. The road was rutted, the pavement cracked and overgrown. In some places, it was more weeds than road.

"Looks like nobody's been around here in a long time," Joe said.

"Wrong." Frank pointed ahead of them. "See those weeds? Something came through here and squashed them all down."

"Something like a car?" Joe said.

Frank nodded. "Let's hope it turns out to be Denny's car."

They bounced farther along the road, until they came to the rusty remains of a chain-link fence. It wouldn't keep anyone out now. Some of the fence poles were completely gone, and in places the fence sagged right to the ground.

The gateposts were still up, but the gates themselves hung off at drunken angles. Frank let the van roll very slowly into the plant parking lot. The concrete there was in even worse shape than that on the road.

"It's like some sort of weird garden," Joe said, staring at clumps of weeds that rose up as high as his head. Some of them looked like young trees.

Frank hit the brakes. "Over there. A flash of gray among all those weeds."

They drove over and pulled up beside a weed patch. Hidden behind it was Denny Payson's gray car.

"Well, now we know he's here," Joe said.

"And we know he doesn't want everyone to know it." Frank was already examining the shell of the plant building. He remembered watching the fire on television. The flames had billowed out the front windows, until the metal Crowell Chemical sign had twisted off.

The scorched, melted sign was a pile of red flakes now. And the front wall of the building had completely fallen in. There was no trace of a roof. It was probably a pile of ash left on the floor inside—whatever hadn't been blown all over town.

Frank remembered reading that parts of the plant had been found miles away.

"Come on," he said to Joe. "Let's go in."

Frank picked a big open hole, ducked his head, and walked inside. Joe was right behind him.

The outside of the wrecked plant looked bizarre enough. But inside it was like something out of a bad science-fiction movie. Heat, explosions, and weird chemical reactions had rearranged everything in the building. Big mixing vats had been turned into huge misshapen blobs of metal. Parts of the floor had apparently been dissolved.

For a second Frank thought back to the day when all this wreckage had happened. It would have taken a pretty brave man to go in and try to rescue the workers. Even if the disaster had been his fault.

Would Denny Payson ever believe that?

They walked around a fallen beam. "Hey, Denny?" Joe called. "It's us, Joe and Frank Hardy. Want to come out and talk?"

The only answer they got was silence.

Joe scowled. "Of course, he wouldn't want to do this the easy way." He raised his voice. "Come on, stop fooling around. We know you're here. We're parked beside your car."

They walked farther into the building, calling Denny's name.

"You know, we're going to feel pretty stupid if he sneaks out and drives away," Joe said.

"Don't worry about that," a voice above them said.

The Hardys whirled around. Standing on what

was left of the building's second floor was Denny Payson.

Frank didn't need much to know Denny wasn't happy to see them.

The glittering pistol braced in Denny's hands told him that, and a whole lot more.

Chapter

13

"DOWN," DENNY PAYSON ordered. "On the ground. Sit on your hands."

Frank and Joe didn't really have a choice. The heavy Colt was trained on them. Slowly they lowered themselves to the ground, tucking their hands under their legs.

"I learned that from watching TV," Denny said. "Everybody makes their captives sit that way. It's supposed to be almost impossible to get back on your feet very quickly."

Denny grinned as he started working his way down to them, using the fallen beam as a rough ladder. But it wasn't a friendly grin, and his gun remained trained on them all the way down.

"I suppose my mom told you I'd be here," Denny said when he finally reached the ground.

He stood over them, but not too close. Not close enough for Frank or Joe to lash out and bring him down.

"This was my secret place, you know," Denny went on. "My mom is the only one who knows about it. She hated the idea of my coming here. Partly it was fear that the building would fall on me, I think." He smiled. "And, of course, she was afraid of what it would do to my mind."

He shook his head. "You know what I used to do here? I'd bring my old plinking gun and shoot at cans. Just like my dad and I used to do. I guess it made me feel he wasn't completely gone—Don't," Denny suddenly said. He aimed his gun at Joe, who had been trying to edge closer to him while he made his speech.

Joe sat very still.

"Denny—" Frank said.

But Denny ran right over his words. "Know what I've been doing here now?" he asked. "Target practice."

He pointed to a row of cans set up on some pieces of torn and pockmarked concrete. "My firing range away from home. Actually, I was testing out something I'd read in a gun magazine. Sort of a New Wave pistol silencer."

Denny kicked something between the Hardys—an empty two-liter soda bottle. It was discolored and had a hole in its bottom.

"That's your basic hardware," Denny explained. "A big plastic bottle. Of course, you have to weaken the load in your bullets, too, so they don't make as big a bang."

"Which is easy enough for you, with your own reloading machine," Frank said.

Denny nodded. "You got it, Frank. It's really impressive. Hardly more than a *pop* when the gun goes off. But the bullets still move fast enough to do their job."

His face was grim. "It was just going to be an experiment, you know. A little reloading project. I had the forty-five shells fixed up a month ago and was waiting to borrow a friend's gun to see if the silencer really worked. Just for the fun of it."

He laughed bitterly. "Then, what luck on my birthday! I got a forty-five Army Colt from my mother. A laser sight from Crowell. And I find out the last five years are a lie. That the man who's been helping our family is the one who got my father killed."

Denny took a deep breath. "I've been a good shot for as long as I can remember. A winner at the sport of shooting." He smiled. "You know, I was never a hunter. I never felt like one. It was always a game. I've never shot at anything alive. Only at bottles or targets. And now I've got a gun, bullets, a silencer, and a reason to use them."

"You can't shoot Lucius Crowell," Frank said. "Even if he did let this place burn down."

"It's not like he lit a match, you know," Joe added. "And he did try to save everyone."

"But he didn't save everyone, did he?" Denny said. "He killed my father, just as surely as if he'd dropped him in one of the acid vats over there." Denny jerked his head toward one of the melted monstrosities in the corner.

"Oh, I know, he's spent five years trying to make it up to me. Our house. Money. Presents. He used to take me to shooting meets, getting me interested in the sport. He was even encouraging me to take up chemistry, so I could work for his company. That's how I recognized the chemicals he was keeping here, and what they would do if any ever got mixed together."

His hand was white on the grip of his gun. "It's lucky some of the stuff wound up in the bay. Otherwise, the whole town might have been blown off the map. It taught him a big lesson. Now he's got the safest plant in the country. *Now,* when it's too late. Well, he can try to make it up for five years or for five centuries. *He won't bring my father back*—and he's going to pay for it!"

"Denny—" Joe tried to calm his friend, but Denny wasn't even listening.

"And now he's running for supervisor on his record as a hero—and because he has such clean hands. The *Times* said as much in the Sunday editorials. Everybody I know is ready to vote for him." He laughed again. "Hey, *I* was going to vote for him until my eyes were opened."

Denny stared down at the Hardys. "You and I know the truth about Lucius Crowell. He's a killer, and he'll kill anyone who tries to tell the real story about him. Look what happened to Steve Vittorio."

He shuddered. "Vittorio was the one witness who wasn't afraid of Crowell. Back when the disaster happened, he started talking about safety violations. He got fired, and he couldn't get a decent job in Bayport. When I tracked him down in Philadelphia, Crowell had him killed."

"We don't think Crowell was in on that," Frank said. "It's his security chief—"

"George Swayne," Denny said. "He's in this whole thing up to his neck."

"Maybe over his head," Frank went on. "He's going beyond Crowell's orders. Beating you up. Killing Vittorio. Trying to kill us—"

"He messed up at the construction site," Joe said. "His first shot at the cable missed, and went into a bag of concrete. We've told the Philadelphia police, and they're looking for it."

Joe shifted around, trying to get some feeling into his hands, and found himself looking down the muzzle of Denny's gun.

"So, *maybe* if they find the bullet, *maybe*

they'll be able to nail George. And I suppose you'll tell me that *maybe* he'll talk, and take Crowell down too.''

Denny's fingers were white as he gripped his pistol. ''Well, *maybe*s aren't enough for me. I'm going to see Crowell go down. Because I'm going to make it happen.''

''Denny, you can't do it that way,'' Joe said desperately.

''No?'' Denny turned on him. ''That's the way you guys do things. What about that terrorist guy who killed your girlfriend? I remember the stories in the papers. You nailed him after a big fight in the mall. If it's all right for you to waste the guy who murdered your girlfriend, why can't I take care of the man who killed my father?''

''I didn't kill Al-Rousasa,'' Joe said. ''He was on the top level of the mall, trying to assassinate a presidential candidate who was speaking below. I tried to stop him before he could shoot, and in the fight, he went over the railing. In fact, before he fell, I tried to save him.''

''If he hadn't tried to kill Joe, he'd still be alive,'' Frank said. ''Instead, he fell to his death.''

Joe's voice was tired as he went on. ''Let me tell you something. I hated that guy, but I don't feel any better because he's dead. It still didn't bring Iola back.''

"How would you feel if he'd gone to court and gotten off?" Denny wanted to know. "That's what's happening with the grand jury. Listen to this."

He pulled out a small radio and flipped it to the local all-news station. They caught the weather forecast, then the announcer said, "And now, back to our live coverage of the grand jury proceedings with Jane Taylor. Jane?"

"Thank you, Phil," the reporter's voice came out of the tinny speaker. "This whole afternoon has been a lesson in how hard it is to investigate a case that's five years old. Papers are missing, important witnesses have died, and a lot of people have just forgotten what happened at the Crowell Chemical plant."

"Or they're just afraid to remember," Denny growled.

"One odd note is that the young man whose accusations sparked this investigation has not been seen in the courtroom all day. Many people are wondering if there's any proof at all to back up those charges. Certainly, Lucius Crowell is confident that the case will come up empty. He's scheduling a news conference for six, in an hour's time, on the steps of the courthouse, where he'll make a public statement. Until then, this is Jane Taylor—"

Denny killed the radio. "Looks like your

friends in Philadelphia didn't find that bullet. But Crowell's made my job easier."

He gestured with his gun. "All right, both of you, keys out of your pockets. Throw them over to me."

Staring at him, Frank and Joe obeyed his order.

Denny knelt to pick up the keys and waggled his gun at Joe when he tried to move. "Don't do anything stupid now, Joe. I'll let you up in a second, after I've got your car keys."

He dropped the keys in his pocket, his gun still on the Hardys. "Okay, get up. And do it very slowly."

The Hardys got stiffly to their legs as Denny stepped back.

"Now I've got to figure out someplace to keep you two," Denny said. "Long enough so you can't stop me."

He pointed at a large vat that looked miraculously undamaged. "That should take care of it," he said. "Through this old inspection hatch."

Again, the Hardys had no choice. They stepped through the hatch. "I won't lock this," Denny said from outside. "But I'll brace something against the door. You'll get out soon enough. I'll just have a comfortable head start. Now step back. I don't want you trying anything stupid, like a rush for the door when my back is turned."

Joe stepped back, a scowl on his face. That was exactly what he'd had in mind.

Frank looked around their new prison. The metal walls were deeply discolored with scaly greenish stains. "I wonder what they used to keep in here."

"Better not to know," Joe said. "But did you notice? There were no weeds growing anywhere near this thing."

"Denny!" Frank yelled through the doorway. "You still have time to give up this crazy idea!"

"No way!" Denny's voice floated back. "By the time you get out of here, Lucius Crowell will be a dead man."

He kicked the door shut, and then something clanged down to hold it in place.

The movement sent the vat walls vibrating, and some of the green scales disintegrated. They floated down in clouds of dust.

Joe was banging on the door as the greenish haze enveloped him. He began coughing and his eyes started to tear.

"What is this stuff?" he asked, wheezing.

Frank began to cough too. "I don't know," he said. "But it's a real killer!"

Chapter

14

EVEN THOUGH HE didn't know for sure that Denny was gone, Joe ran to the entrance hatch. He pushed against it gently. It didn't budge. Joe braced himself and pushed harder. The hatch still didn't move.

Joe muttered something, then threw himself against the door. He bounced back, rubbing his shoulder. The door rattled, and the whole wall shook.

A new shower of scales came down, turning into a hazy cloud. It drifted around Joe, who immediately began coughing and choking. He staggered back, clutching at his throat, unable to catch his breath.

Tears streaming from his eyes, Joe retreated

from the cloud. He was almost bent double, still coughing uncontrollably.

Frank knelt down, trying to support his brother, staring worriedly at Joe's red, twisted face. And still his coughing continued without any break.

A wisp of dust floated by, making Frank's eyes sting. He finally got Joe over to the far end of the vat, away from the green dust.

At last his coughing subsided, and Joe was able to suck some air into his aching lungs.

"Wha-what *is* that stuff?" Joe finally managed in a hoarse voice.

"I don't know," Frank answered. "But we have a big problem. Denny thought he was just slowing us up by putting us in here. But he's actually stuck us in a perfect trap. We've got to knock the door down to get out of here. And every time we hit it, we get another dose of that dust."

"*We?*" Joe said. "So far, I've been the one choking my head off."

"That's because you jumped in without thinking," Frank said. He pulled a handkerchief out of his back pocket and tied it around his face. "I hope you've got one of these things, and not a bunch of crumpled tissues."

Joe grinned as he pulled out a handkerchief of his own. "We look like bandits getting ready to rob the stage in a western movie."

Frank's eyes twinkled over his mask. "Whatcha say, pardner?" he asked in a long drawl. "Let's bust out of here."

Together, they dashed for the door, hitting it. But it stood up to them. The only thing their combined attack did was to bring down more of the green flakes.

They kept on smashing into the door in spite of the tears running down their cheeks. But the fine green dust made its way right through their handkerchief masks. Soon they were both convulsed in helpless coughing spasms. They had to crawl along the ground to reach fresh air.

When he could finally speak again, Joe turned to Frank. "Well, that was certainly good thinking. I think this was the worst choking fit I've had yet."

Frank glared at him.

"I mean, that *was* the plan, wasn't it?" Joe went on.

"Funny man," croaked Frank, starting to unbutton his shirt.

"What's this?" Joe asked. "Are we going to have a fight? A couple rounds of boxing?"

Frank shook his head. "We're going to try it again. With heavier masks, this time." He wrapped the shirt around his face, getting several layers of cloth around his mouth and nose.

Joe took off his shirt and imitated Frank.

"You ready to try again?" Frank's voice was muffled under wrappings on his face.

"I feel like the whole Bayport defensive line is dancing on my lungs." Joe got to his feet. "Let's get this over with."

He got shakily to his feet. "Come on."

They charged into the green cloud, which still hadn't settled. As their weight hit the door, Frank felt the hatch shift a little.

"It's moving!" he yelled.

"Great," came Joe's muffled voice. "Because I can't see it."

More of the green scales came down in a landslide, and the green cloud became too thick to see through. They kept pounding on the door, until the killer dust made its way through the layers of their new masks.

Joe was paralyzed with great racking coughs. He couldn't pound anymore. He was just clinging to the door, trying to remain upright. Half-blinded by tears and dust, Frank led him back to clearer air.

He made Joe lie down. Then Frank charged back into the green cloud, throwing his whole body into a karate kick.

Frank's foot slammed into the door. From outside, metal screeched against metal. The door gave an inch, then stuck again. The entire side of the vat shook like a giant gong. But they still couldn't get out.

Frank was sagging against the door, defeated, when a piece of metal fell on his shoulder. It was about the size of a dinner plate, and it hurt as it bounced off his shoulder and hit the ground.

Frank searched blindly for it with his hands, hoping he could use it as a tool to wedge the door open. But as he picked the piece up, he could feel the edge flaking away. It had been eaten away, it was too weak—

Too weak! Trying to hold his breath, Frank staggered out of the cloud again. There was very little fresh air left in the vat now. Most of it was filled with drifting green motes. Joe was breathing raggedly, flapping his shirt to keep the green cloud away.

"What have you got there?" he asked.

"A piece of the vat," Frank answered. "It nearly fell on my head." He showed Joe the flaky green edge on the metal.

"Looks like this green rust or whatever ate it away," Joe said.

Frank nodded. "And that's our way out of here. Let's find a big green patch at ground level."

They looked around the little area where the air was clear, but there were no patches of green rust. Frank and Joe looked at each other, took a deep breath, then headed back into the killer cloud.

Each of them worked along an opposite wall of the vat. The green dust whirled in front of Frank's eyes, obscuring everything as he picked his way along the wall. He was working by touch because his eyes were burning so badly, he had shut them. His lungs were burning, too, so he held his breath.

Then his questing hands came across a large scaly patch on the wall. He opened his eyes and peered closely at the wall. Yes, it was the green corrosion. And the patch seemed large enough for them to fit through.

"Joe!" he called. "Over here!" Frank grimaced and spat as the dust got into his mouth. The stuff even *tasted* bad. "Come on!"

Joe's voice came out of the dust cloud. "Where?" He was beginning to cough again.

"Follow my voice!" The dust was getting to Frank too. He pulled his shirt tighter over his nose and mouth, but even so, the green particles started him hacking.

A figure appeared, shambling blindly through the cloud, zeroing in on Frank's coughing. "Good guiding," Joe gasped as he reached his brother. "I could hear that cough all the way on the other side."

Through teary eyes, they examined the rust patch before them. Then they started kicking at it. A fresh cloud of dust enveloped them, but they held their breath and kept kicking.

What if the metal hasn't been weakened enough? Frank wondered. What if we can't get through? He knew that this fresh cloud of dust would be enough to fill the old vat. If they couldn't get out, they'd have created their own gas chamber.

The thought of that made him kick harder.

Frank drew back his leg, sending another power kick into the patch of corrosion. His foot jarred against the weakened metal and then, it went through!

Joe joined his brother, kicking around the edges of the hole. Together, they knocked larger chunks of the wall loose. The dust cloud was too dense to see through, but they kept on kicking, in spite of their blind stares and coughs. At last they escaped into fresh air, stumbling into the sunlight.

"Kicking my way through a metal wall makes me feel like a comic-book hero." Joe tried to flex a muscle, but ruined the effect when he started to cough again.

"Yeah? Well, come on, Superguy. We still have to catch up with Denny."

Frank's words wiped the smile off Joe's face. "Right. Let's get going."

They raced to the van. "I thought he'd do something clever, like shoot out the tires," Joe said, stopping to check.

He stopped when he heard Frank pounding

on the steering wheel. "He didn't have to," his brother said. "He took the car key."

Joe came around to the front of the van. "Yeah, but we've got an extra set—"

"He thought of that, too," Frank said with disgust. "So he broke the key off in the ignition. I can't get the key out, or the engine started."

Joe leaned under the wheel. "More over," he ordered his brother. "There's more than one way to skin a Denny."

He went to work, pulling wires and using a wrench to break the ignition lock. Suddenly, the engine roared to life.

"One hot-wired van at your service," Joe said, letting Frank take the steering wheel again. "Just do me one favor. Don't let the engine die out whenever you stop. The cops might get a little suspicious if I have to do this operation in the middle of the street."

He ran around and hauled himself aboard, and Frank took off. "Be careful on the bumps," Joe warned. "We don't want to jiggle those wires loose."

"All right, all right, I'll save the speed for smoother roads," Frank said. He reached out to turn on the radio, but Joe grabbed his hand.

"Sorry. We lost that connection."

"Great," Frank fumed. "Without the news, we won't know when the grand jury lets out."

"They aren't supposed to knock off before

six." Joe checked his watch. "We should get there in time."

"If they don't finish early." Frank sighed. "Let's just hope some of the witnesses are long-winded."

As they drove toward town, the already cloudy sky darkened. Then came a sprinkle of raindrops, which quickly turned into a downpour.

"Just what we need," Frank said, turning to Joe. "Did you kill our windshield wipers too?"

"They should work," Joe said as his brother's hand went to the control. "I hope."

The showers stopped after a few minutes. However, the roads were still slippery and sent the Hardys into one scary skid.

Frank steered them out of it, and then they were in the town, heading for Main Street.

The Bayport courthouse was just off the town square, a big red-brick building with an old-fashioned copper dome. On sunny days, the polished copper glittered like gold. But under that day's gray and overcast sky, it just looked drab and wet.

The other outstanding feature of the courthouse was the white stone staircase that led up to the front of the building. As a kid, Frank had always been impressed by the number of steps it took to reach the door. Now he was wondering if they would be the stage for Denny to shoot Crowell.

Even from a block away, the Hardys could see that a pretty good crowd had assembled on those steps. There were many Crowell supporters on hand, as well as press people and two TV crews.

The crowd began to cheer as the courthouse doors opened. Lucius Crowell started down the stairs, with George holding an umbrella over his head.

"He's coming out!" Frank said, braking the van to a stop. Both he and Joe frantically scanned the crowd, looking for a tall kid with red hair.

He didn't seem to be anywhere in the mob on the steps. But then a spear of brilliant red light flashed across the street, right in front of their windshield.

It painted a round red dot of light—right on Lucius Crowell's chest.

Chapter

15

As SOON AS Frank saw the beam flashing in front of him, he stepped hard on the gas. The van lurched forward, taking them straight into the laser.

It felt weird to see the beam come through the windshield and weirder still to realize they were passing right through the line of fire. If Denny should pull the trigger right then, both Hardy brothers would buy it.

But the instant of danger passed. Now the van's solid metal sides were between Denny and Crowell. Frank hit the brakes, leaving the van right where it was.

"You stop Denny," he told Joe, opening his door. "I've got to get to Crowell."

He dashed across the street and up the courthouse stairs. It wasn't easy getting through the tightly packed mob.

The crowd was milling around nervously. Both the newspeople and Crowell's supporters were wondering what was going on.

"He's been shot!" somebody yelled, apparently thinking the spot of red on Crowell's chest was blood.

Frank heard the response as he pushed his way deeper into the crowd. "What are you, stupid? It was only a light. Something to do with the TV cameras, I think."

Everyone was waiting for an explanation from Lucius Crowell. He stepped forward to speak just as Frank was reaching the front ranks of the mob.

Crowell stood frozen for a moment, half-leaning against George, his face white. Frank knew just how terrible a shock that unexpected bolt of red light had been. He couldn't have enjoyed suddenly finding himself a target.

But Lucius Crowell hid the strain as he began speaking. He even managed to turn it into a joke. "I'm afraid that's a little too small for a spotlight," he said. "And red never was my color."

That got a laugh from the crowd.

"It's really nothing to worry about," Crowell went on. "Just a little harassment. I've gotten used to it in the last few days."

The Crowell supporters in the crowd were cheering now. But George's actions were the exact opposite of Crowell's calming words. He was standing beside his chief, scanning the crowd, trying to spot Denny. His eyes kept straying back to the Hardys' black van, conspicuously double parked across the street. Frank also noticed that George's jacket was open, and one hand stayed firmly on his gun.

"Frank!" a voice in his ear drowned out Crowell's speech. Turning, Frank found himself standing next to Barbara Lynch. "Mrs. Payson wouldn't come to the hearings with us. She's staying at home until she hears something about Denny."

She grabbed his arm. "I was so scared when I heard he'd disappeared. Is he okay? Did you find him?"

"He was in Philadelphia." Frank quickly brought her up to date.

"So he *is* around here—with his gun." Barbara began to shudder. "We didn't know what to think when we saw that laser. Callie thought that maybe it was a plant, that Crowell was going to fake an attack on himself to gain sympathy."

"Where is Callie?" Frank asked, scanning the crowd while he talked with the girl.

"Well, she wasn't sure she was right." Barbara's shakes got worse as she tried to contain her tears. "So she went to get the cops."

Even as Barbara was speaking, the courthouse doors opened. Framed in them was Callie Shaw. And right beside her was Con Riley and his partner.

Callie pointed straight at the Hardys' van. Con and the other policeman started down the stairs, steering wide of the political hoopla.

"Oh, Frank!" Barbara was crying openly now. "What are they going to do to Denny?"

Joe Hardy's thoughts were almost the same. What is Denny going to do to me?

While Frank had run across the street, Joe had barely pulled on the handle of the van door before he found himself facing trouble.

To be specific, he found himself facing the muzzle of Denny's gun. Or rather, he was facing the end of the weird silencer rig that Denny had set up.

It should have been laughable—a two-liter bottle screwed to the end of a pistol. But Joe didn't find it funny. He remembered the way George's bullet had torn through the bottle in his hand that day back at Denny's house. And then there were the practice bottles Denny had used to test his silencer. Joe could still see the stained insides, the sharp-edged holes in the bottom.

No, this weapon was nothing to laugh at, even

if it did look like a reject from a science-fiction movie.

Joe forced his eyes from the gun to the boy holding it. Denny's hand was shaking a little. That wasn't a good sign. Joe knew only too well how delicate the trigger was on an automatic. The slightest pressure, and *bang!*

He took a deep breath. "Nice outfit, Denny."

Dressed in jeans and a trench coat, Denny did look odd. But he wasn't completely out of place on a street that had just seen a rainstorm a few minutes before.

Of course Joe knew the real reason for the long coat. Denny had needed something to hide his unwieldy weapon.

"You—you got out of that vat a lot earlier than I expected." Denny finally got the words out between clenched teeth.

"No thanks to you," Joe said. "There was some kind of leftover gunk in there that nearly killed us."

Denny frowned. "It was only meant to slow you down." He looked apologetic for a moment. Then he moved the gun minutely in line with Joe's head.

"I suppose Frank is off getting the cops. You had to ruin everything. I had it all set up. Just stand quietly in this doorway until Crowell comes out. Pull this rig out from under my coat, *pop!* and have it back under before anybody even turned around." Denny was sweating and his hand was still shaking.

"You don't have to do it, Denny," Joe pleaded. "Let the law—"

"I'm going to do it to him," Denny whispered fiercely. "No one's going to stop me now. Not you, not the cops."

"Rubfriblath," Joe mumbled, his head sagging in defeat.

"What was that?" Denny took a step forward.

Joe was ready for it. He threw his weight against the already open door. It swung around, slamming into Denny.

His gun went off harmlessly into the air. Just as he'd said, there was only a gentle *pop* that couldn't be heard a few feet away.

Joe jumped out of the van, trying to pin Denny down. But Denny wriggled free, leaving Joe with the belt from his trench coat grasped in his hands.

Denny skittered backward along the sidewalk, trying to get up. He flinched as Joe threw the belt in his face. Before he could pull himself together, Joe was on him, grabbing the gun, trying to wrestle it away.

They struggled in silence for a moment, each of them trying to point the awkward weapon away from himself.

Then Denny suddenly threw himself forward, butting Joe with his forehead.

137

Joe fell backward, desperately trying to keep some kind of grip on the gun. His hand slid along the hot barrel, then caught at the neck of the soda bottle.

The bottle popped loose, and Joe fell flat on his back.

Denny reeled back, too, caught by surprise. But he recovered quickly. He was on his feet before Joe could get his legs under him.

So Joe didn't try to get up. He tried to knock Denny down. His wild kick caught Denny in the side of the knee, sending him staggering.

Joe jumped and caught Denny around the waist. Denny used the gun as a club.

The butt came crashing down on Joe's shoulder, but he gritted his teeth and held on. He ignored the pain when the gun came down on his head.

They staggered drunkenly along the side of the van, Denny struggling to stay upright, Joe trying to take him down.

A new flash of pain, too strong to ignore, came as the gun's grip slashed along Joe's cheek. Then he caught it on the side of the head, and the whole world went red and hazy.

Joe's arms suddenly seemed to be made of wet cardboard. Denny broke his grip easily and pulled himself to the front of the van. Joe started to fall down, as if in slow motion. Yet somehow he couldn't get an arm out to break the fall, and he hit the ground hard.

For a moment, blackness threatened to swallow up the red.

Groaning, Joe rolled over on the ground. The world was coming back into focus a little now. He could make out some shapes.

Then he realized what he was seeing. Denny was leaning across the front of the van, steadying his hands to aim his gun.

Joe couldn't quite remember what Denny was aiming at, but he knew he couldn't let Denny shoot.

He dragged himself along the gutter, unable even to get to his knees. The world kept zooming in and out of focus. Sometimes Denny seemed miles away, other times he was right on top of Joe.

So, it came as a shock when Joe bumped into Denny's feet.

Denny jumped in surprise and looked down. He kicked away the hands that were feebly grabbing for his ankles.

Joe made a supreme effort to get up. Got to stop him, he thought. Got to!

He managed to push up on one arm, bringing himself to the level of Denny's knees. That, he realized, was as high as he could get.

Joe threw himself in a wobbly tackle and fell into blackness.

Chapter

16

LUCIUS CROWELL HAD just finished his speech. He was basking in the applause of his audience, his arms thrown wide, when the laser stabbed at his chest again.

A gasp rose from a dozen throats as the crowd turned. This time they all saw Denny Payson sprawled across the front of the black van, aiming his gun.

Frank just felt sick. What had happened to Joe?

The whole thing couldn't have happened at a worse time. Con Riley and his partner were still coming down the stairs, and the bulk of the crowd was between them and Denny. They had their guns out, but they didn't dare shoot.

George's cannon was also in his hand. He had

no scruples about shooting around innocent people. But Lucius Crowell hissed something at him that stopped George from taking aim.

Frank turned back to watch Denny. Where was Joe?

He got his answer an instant later, as Denny looked back and down. The laser's red dot moved around for a second. Joe was obviously with Denny. And he must need help.

Barbara Lynch took advantage of Denny's temporary distraction. She climbed up the stairs until she was standing directly in front of Lucius Crowell. The red dot from the laser stood out brilliantly on the white dress she was wearing.

Barbara turned around. "Denny!" she yelled. "Stop it. *Please!*"

When Denny looked up and saw his own girlfriend shielding Crowell, he went pale. "Get out of the way!" he screamed up at Barbara. "He's a murderer. Why are you defending him?"

"Because I don't want you to be a murderer too," she shouted back.

The cops had used the interruption to reach the edges of the crowd. They were free to start firing now, if they needed to.

Maybe Crowell noticed this and wanted to head off a war. Or maybe he felt he had to show that he could control the situation. He started talking in a loud, booming voice.

"Dennis, please be sensible. You're getting nowhere with this crazy campaign of yours. Give it up. If you turn yourself in, I promise—"

"Oh, so now I'm crazy, am I?" Denny's hands were shaking so badly, the laser dot jiggled all around Barbara.

Frank decided it was just as well. If he'd really pulled himself together, Denny might have tried for a head shot at Crowell. And he might just have made it.

"And why should I trust any promise that *you* might make?" Denny went on.

Crowell kept his smooth politician's face on, but he reeled as if he'd been struck. For the first time, someone was taking Lucius Crowell apart. And the fact that the person doing the job was the closest thing Crowell had to a son didn't make it any easier for him to hold things together.

"If you're going to attack my honesty, you should bring facts, not accusations." Crowell's voice sounded angry now. Frank smiled grimly. If this was worked in the right way—

"Those are pretty brave words, for a man who's hiding behind a girl," Frank suddenly shouted. "Clean hands? What about a little backbone?"

They had definitely cracked Crowell's armor. He tried to hold back, but he couldn't help himself. "If you and your friends are going to throw childish insults at me, the sooner we bring this to an end, the better. Put down that gun, and I'll make sure—"

"Another promise?" Denny yelled. "You must think I'm really stupid."

"I've never broken a promise to anyone in this town," Crowell said angrily.

Denny laughed bitterly. "That's easy enough, when all the people you broke your promises to are dead. You promised my dad you would run a safe plant. *And where is my father now?*"

"You can't go trying to blame someone for an accident—" Crowell began.

"It's some accident, when six people wind up dead," Denny said.

"Now, Dennis," Crowell said. He was trying to sound like the voice of reason, but Frank could hear the triumph in his tone. "You're getting completely carried away now. Everyone knows that only five—"

"You're out of date, Mr. Crowell," Frank spoke up again. "Six people have died in this mess. Five in the disaster and Steve Vittorio. He died today in Philadelphia. Maybe you'd like to call that an accident too. Somebody shot away the ropes on a crane and dropped a ton of concrete blocks on him."

Doubtful muttering started up in the crowd when they heard this.

But more importantly, Crowell's mask completely broke. He turned in horror to stare at George Swayne. His reaction told Frank that George hadn't reported what had gone down in Philadelphia.

Better yet, all of this was happening before the whirring TV cameras. Frank continued pressing his advantage.

"Even more interesting, whoever shot out those cables used a laser sight."

By now the crowd had begun to get agitated. Frank raised his voice over the wild chatter. "I know what these people are thinking, but my brother and I saw Denny Payson just before those blocks came down. He was close enough that they nearly hit him, and he didn't have a gun in his hand."

He pointed at the chrome cannon that George still had out. "But we might all notice that your security chief has a gun with a laser sight." Above the shining metal of the pistol, the black box of the sight stood out boldly.

George quickly stuffed the gun under his jacket. "Now listen, you punk kid—" he began.

"Maybe you can tell us where you spent the afternoon." Frank decided that it was time to gamble. "We can get a witness to say you discovered that Steve Vittorio had gone to Philadelphia."

George's face showed that he'd forgotten about the old custodian.

"And, of course, there's the physical evidence you left at the scene of the crime," Frank went on.

"You never found that bullet!" George yelled. Then he realized that everyone was staring at him, including his own boss.

"I, uh, mean—" He raised his hands, trying to find something to say to the suddenly hostile crowd.

"Look, you're not going to blame all this on me." George turned to Lucius Crowell. "I worked as your bag man to grease a few palms, making things easier for the plant. And I helped cover things up when everything went wrong. But you were the boss. You were always the boss."

Lucius Crowell moved fast. He reached under George's jacket and snatched the gun out of its clamshell holster. Then he grabbed Barbara's windbreaker, keeping her in front of him as a shield.

The gun stayed aimed at George Swayne. "You go off on your own. You shoot at people. Beat them up. Kill them. And then you try to worm out of it, to blame it all on *me*—"

Crowell's finger tightened on the trigger.

Frank held his breath.

He'd cracked the case wide open. But had he also managed to get someone killed?

Chapter

17

EVERYONE'S EYES WERE on the pistol in Crowell's hand. They gasped as the hammer clicked back. Suddenly a dot of red appeared on the frame of the big pistol. Denny's laser!

Then came a flat crack! The gun went flying from Crowell's fingers.

He yelled and shook his stinging hand.

Con and his partner were already running up the stairs. Crowell and George both went for the gun. With his stiff leg, Crowell was at a disadvantage bending for the pistol.

George had his hand on the gun when a foot came down on his wrist. "Sorry, George," Frank said. "You won't be needing that anymore."

The police moved in then to take charge.

"Frank!" Callie came running down the stairs. "You got them. Where's Joe? And what happened to Barbara?"

They both turned to see Barbara pushing her way through the crowd, heading down the stairs toward the van and Denny.

Callie and Frank began working their way toward her. They were right behind Barbara as she ran across the street.

Denny was still slumped across the front of the van. He stared at the gun in his hands as if he'd never seen it before.

Barbara rushed up to him, reaching for his hands.

But Denny stepped back, looking down at the ground behind him. As Frank and Callie came up, they saw him kneeling down beside Joe. "I'm sorry," he kept saying. "I must have been crazy."

Denny hit the magazine release, sending his ammunition clip to the ground. He worked the action of the gun, jacking the last bullet out. His fingers moved mechanically, in actions he had practiced a million times.

Then he took the gun and put it in Joe's fumbling hand. "I should've let you take it in the first place," Denny said.

"If you had, you might not have had time to make that shot," Frank said. "You managed to save both Crowell and George."

Denny shook his head. "I saw him about to make the biggest mistake of his life," he said. "And I couldn't let him do it. There's been enough killing."

He looked up at Frank. "I guess the cops will want my gun," he said, shrugging. "The important thing is to get Joe to a hospital. I hit him pretty hard."

Frank came down to take one of Joe's arms. Together, they got Joe up and turned to meet the advancing police.

A little while later Frank and Callie were helping a still-rocky Joe out of the Bayport hospital. They stopped in surprise when they saw Denny and Barbara waiting for them at the entrance.

Denny looked a little embarrassed as he asked, "Um, how're you feeling, Joe?"

Joe grinned. "Like someone ran my brain through a food processor—and then poured it back in through my ear." He shook his head, then winced. "No, I'm okay. Just a headache. They don't even think I've got a concussion."

He touched the scrape on his cheek, which was already starting to turn beautiful colors. "We're going to have matching bruises though. Maybe we'll start a trend for the good-looking guys in Bayport."

"Yeah," said Callie. "Real manly."

Denny ran a finger along his own bruised cheek. "I took some lumps on this case," he said. "And I'm sorry I gave you some too. If I'd listened to you guys, maybe we could have avoided some of this.

"You were right, you know. I had Crowell dead in my sights. But I knew—it just wasn't—enough."

Joe sighed, his eyes filled with the pain of loss. "I know what you mean."

"What did the police have to say?" Callie asked, trying to change the subject.

"They've arrested George for the murder of Steve Vittorio. After they played the videotapes from the TV cameras, they called the Philadelphia cops. That bullet had just been found." Denny looked grim.

"What about Lucius Crowell?" Frank asked gently.

"Obviously he's given up the race for supervisor," Barbara said. "And he's giving the cops all the help he can about the disaster at the plant, and the cover-up. He says he should never have kept those chemicals there in the first place. But he swears he didn't know about what George was doing. And I believe him."

"So do I. You know, he thanked me for shooting the gun out of his hand." Denny's eyes were almost dazed as he spoke. "He said he understood the way I felt when I came after him, and he's glad I stopped him.''

"I guess he's not an easy man to understand,'' Frank said. "He went along with a slimy deal that led to disaster, but he did risk his life to save people in the fire. I believe he didn't know what George was doing to protect him.''

Then Frank changed the subject. "How about you, Denny?'' he asked. "What did the police say to you?''

Denny shrugged. "They're talking about a concealed weapons charge—''

"What weapon?'' Joe asked.

Denny blinked, a little worried. "Well, my gun, of course—''

"That wasn't concealed. You had it right out in the open—I saw it!'' He started laughing, and the others joined in.

"I think there's a good chance for you getting off pretty easy,'' Joe said. "The question is, what will you be doing after that?''

"Getting on with my life.'' Denny hugged Barbara. "I finally realized how much I've been living in the past, but that's over. The mystery of what happened to my father is over. And I've got you guys to thank for bringing it to a decent end.''

Frank shrugged, a little embarrassed. "And how about the other passion in your life? Will you keep shooting?''

Denny smiled. "I guess that's up to the police—whether they give me my gun back."

Joe broke in. "Well, if not, let me suggest a sport to you. It's called basketball. There's shooting involved, among other things."

He tried to fake a shot and winced again. "Just keep it in mind. As soon as my head gets better, I'd be happy to teach you."

Frank and Joe's next case:

It's supposed to be a carefree Bermuda vacation for the Hardy brothers with just a little bit of detective work on the side. Between sunbathing and snorkeling they'll investigate local expatriate Bernhard Kruger, who may be involved in a credit card scam. Things heat up fast.

First Frank and Joe's car is run off a cliff into the water. Then, when they try to rent a couple of mopeds with their father's credit card, they're charged with fraud and counterfeiting. With a vicious enemy closing in, Frank and Joe find themselves in some very deep water in *The Number File*, Case #17 in The Hardy Boys Casefiles.